Ishtar

Ruwaida Abd
Enjoy Reading

Ishtar

THE LAST DATE

RUWAIDA ABD

ISBN: 978-1-63901-435-4   (Paperback Edition)
ISBN: 978-1-63901-436-1   (Hardcover Edition)
ISBN: 978-1-63901-428-6   (E-book Edition)

Book Ordering Information

Best Books Media
132 West 31st Street, 1st Fl.
New York, NY, 10001 USA

www.bestbooksmedia.com
Info@bestbooksmedia.com
1 (347) 537-6903

Printed in the United States of America

CONTENTS

Chapter One

THE MEETING

"Are you sure you want to work in a bar." Nazik asked her sister Ishtar when there were in their room sitting on a bed.

"Yes I am." Ishtar said then she added while she was standing "I need another job."

"No, you do not."

Ishtar looked at her "Yes, I do."

"But it will be at night."

"I will work with Maria at the same bar." Ishtar said while she was walking toward a window of their room

"Are you going to start this Friday?"

"Yes I will. I will come back home as soon as I finish working in library, so I can relax for few hours then I will go to my new job." Ishtar explained

"You will be exhausted the next day."

Ishtar looked at her sister "I can relax on Sundays."

"Yea, if mother does not bother you."

"You can tell her I am tired or take her to the church."

"She prefers being with you."

"You are just lazy." Ishtar said then she walked far from her sister while her sister followed her "I am not lazy."

Ishtar looked at her "You do nothing."

"What do I have to do?" Ishtar's sister seemed angry

"You can clean or cook."

"I hate both of them."

"Take her to the church."

"Maybe."

Ishtar left the room angry and disappointed "Stop following me!" Ishtar said to her sister without looking at her

"I said maybe." Ishtar's sister said

"Okay." Ishtar said while she was entering the kitchen room

"Are you going to cook something?"

"No." Ishtar said

"But I am hungry."

Ishtar looked at her and said "You can try cooking." Her sister seemed sad and did not reply.

Ishtar is in her early twenties. She lives in New York City with her mother and younger sister. She worked in many places. First one was in bakery which she stayed there for several months then she worked in kids clothing store as a cashier and in her free time she was volunteering in a library. After months from volunteering she started working there. Although the library is far from her apartment and she has to take three buses and spend an hour and a half from her time but she enjoyed working there.

When her mother got ill and started taking different kinds of medicine, Ishtar decided to have another job to cover the expenses of medication.

On Friday night Ishtar was excited and afraid to start her new job. She prepared herself early and waited for Maria to pick her up and work together. The bar was big. It offers many large screen- televisions for people; also there was a room for people who like to play sport as bowling and billiard.

"This bar is so big." Ishtar said to Maria when they were changing their clothes and wearing a bar's uniform.

"Yes, it is." Maria said then she added "When I started working here televisions where in their places, but sport room has been recently opened."

"I am afraid."

"If you need anything, you just have to tell me."

"Okay, I will."

"You may do not like the job in first days."

"Why?"

"You may be tired or have headache because the noise."

"Maybe."

"You will get used to after working several days."

"Yea, I think I will like it."

"You look beautiful." Maria said to Ishtar while she was smiling

Ishtar looked at her uniform which was a T-shirt and skirt, both in black colour.

"I do not like them." Ishtar said

"Why?"

"I do not like the skirt." Ishtar said

"You look amazing." Maria was trying to comfort her while Ishtar did not respond.

Ishtar and Maria met when Ishtar and her family moved to live in their apartment since that day they become friends.

"You have to be fast and treat the customer nicely. You have to do your best." Maria said while Ishtar was listening carefully and nodding her head.

On that night Ishtar was proud of herself. She was patient with her co- workers and customers. When she arrived home, she was exhausted, and had a headache but she was happy. She got a shower and slept quietly.

Next day, Ishtar could not wake up early, she was so tired

"It is 11 o'clock. Go and check her, maybe she is not well. " Ishtar's mother commanded her younger daughter after she looked at the watch

"She warned me earlier." Ishtar's sister said

"Warned you!" Ishtar's mother was surprise

"Yes."

"Go to the room and wake her up." Ishtar's mother was angry

"Okay, I will." Ishtar's sister said while she was standing. She walked slowly to their room and looked disappointed at her sister. She held a pillow and started screaming and hitting Ishtar's body "Wake up! Wake up now!" Ishtar moved her body and covered her face while he sister sighed and threw the pillow back to the bed

Ruwaida Abd

"It is a sunny day. You have to wake up!............ I do not want to spend my day at home…" Ishtar did not move "I did not eat my breakfast. I am waiting for you to make it for us. I am so hungry."

Ishtar totally ignored her sister and did not move or respond while her sister moved close to Ishtar's bed and bend over "I am not joking. I am waiting for you to make a breakfast."

"Leave me alone" Ishtar said angry while her sister waited in the room looking at Ishtar and hoping to get up from her bed

"Leave me alone, please. I am so tired." Ishtar said

"We are waiting for you." Ishtar's sister said while she was exiting the room

"Why are you screaming?" Ishtar's mother asked her younger daughter when she got into the kitchen

"Ishtar does not want to wake up."

"Is she sick?" Ishtar's mother asked her younger daughter

"No." Ishtar's sister said while she was sitting on a chair "She just does not want to wake up so we will stay hungry."

"Why do not you make the breakfast by yourself."

"I can not and I do not want." Ishtar's sister said while her mother said nothing

After few minutes, Ishtar joined them in the kitchen room

"You finally woke up." Ishtar's sister said

"Yes, I did because of you!"

"My mother told me."

"Yes, I did." Ishtar's mother said while Ishtar was yawning

"I am tired. You should leave me sleeping."

"How was your job last night?" Ishtar's mother asked

"It was good." Ishtar responded

"Why are you tired if it was good?"

"Because I did not have enough sleep."

"What is your job?" her mother asked after second of silence

Ishtar looked at her sister then she said after seconds of hesitating "It is a bakery."

"Oh, I thought you do not like working in bakery."

"It is temporary."

"You have to be careful at night especially you are coming back home very late."

4

"I came home when I finished working."

"You have to be careful."

"I work with Maria."

"Oh, I did not know Maria works in bakery."

Ishtar said "Yes, she does."

Ishtar did not say the truth about her job to her mother because her mother does not allow her to work in a bar with drinker people then comes home very late. As a result Ishtar preferred to keep the truth to herself so her mother won't panic especially she has very bad health

"Can we eat please?" Ishtar's sister asked

"Yes, sure and you have to help me." Ishtar said while she was standing up

"Can you boil some eggs please?" Ishtar's mother asked

"Yes, sure." Ishtar said happily then she opened the fridge and got some eggs while her sister was getting empty cups for coffee

"I asked you to make breakfast."

"I can not cook."

"You are only boiling eggs."

"I want something else."

"Yes, of course." Ishtar seemed angry while her sister looked at her then she asked her while she was handling her a cup of coffee "What time did you come home yesterday?"

"It was dawn."

"Wow, late."

"Yes, and did not let me to sleep."

"I prepared everything."

"Okay, but I am still sleepy."

"Are you working tonight?"

"Yes."

Ishtar's sister sighed "Okay, I will not wake you up."

Ishtar smiled "Good." Then she said sharply "Try to take her to the church."

Ishtar's sister seemed disappointed "I will try."

"Thanks." Ishtar said with a smile

"We need some fruits and vegetables." their mother said

"On Sunday you can buy when Nazik will take you to the church."

"Nazik will take me to the church!" Ishtar's mother was surprise "How?"

Ishtar walked toward her mother while she was holding two plates, one has slices of tomatoes and cucumber another one chopped boiled eggs "Yes, she will." Ishtar set the plates on a table

"Why do not you take me to the church?" Ishtar's mother asked her

Ishtar looked at her mother "I can not."

"Why?"

"I will work Saturday night also."

"Why are you working another job?"

"I want to save money."

"Why do you want to save money?" Ishtar said nothing while her mother added "Financially we are fine. You do not have to work different jobs."

"i will quit if i do not like it." Ishtar walked back

"You will be tired in next day."

"I will be fine." Ishtar responded while she was walking back to her mother and holding bread then she sat beside her

"Why do not you work in morning instead of night?" her mother asked

"As soon as I find another job, I will quit night job." Ishtar explained

"Okay." Ishtar's mother said then she took peice of bread and said "After finish eating I want to go walking."

"I am coming with you." Ishtar's sister said when she was sitting

"What about you?" Ishtar's mother asked her

"I prefer staying home."

"Okay." Her mother said then she started eating

"I have never been here." Jessica said to her brother William when they were inside a car, waiting in front of the bar at Saturday night.

"It is a good place. We will enjoy." William said

"Okay, I hope you will find a spot and we do not wait for so long." Jessica said when she was getting out of the car

"No, we are not going to wait." William said while he was locking the car then he walked together with his sister and his friends to the bar

"It seems good." Julia, who is Jessica's friend, said when they got into the bar

"Yes, it is." Jessica said

The bar was crowded. Some people were watching basketball match while others ultimate fight. William looked around then he walked ahead of them

"I am going to follow him." Julia said to Jessica when they were walking together

"Go and follow him." Jessica said to Julia

"I am." Julia said happily and walked faster toward William while Jessica and her fiancé Mike were following them. They sat on a table which was in a corner of the room. Jessica sat beside her fiancé while William sat beside Julia

"This is not a good spot." Jessica said

"Why?" her fiance asked

"Because both of you will focus on a television."

Mike looked at her "We will not."

"Oh, there is game room." Julia said

"Yes, there is." William said

"Can we play?" Jessica asked

"Yes, we can." Julia said

"You can go to game's room I will stay watching televion here." William said

"Why do you want to stay alone here?" Jessica said

"I am watching."

"We come together here."

"I will join you later."

Julia and Jessica tried to change William's idea but he insisted to stay alone. William dose not have a girlfriend and Julia wants to be his girlfriend and asked Jessica to help her with her plans.

William stayed in his place waiting for them. He was looking at his cell phone when Ishtar asked him "may I help you?"

William raised his head and looked at her face. He knows everyone who works there, but this waitress he is seeing her for the first time.

Ishtar was looking strangely and waiting for his answer.

He looked from head to toe rapidly then said "oh….can you bring four bottles of beer "

Ishtar wrote down on her paper "any thing else."

"For now, only beer."

William looked at Ishtar when she moved and kept her eyes on her until she was gone.

William is 39 years old and successful business man. He worked in several jobs. When he saved some money, started working as business man buying and selling stores, restaurant, and properties. At age of thirty, he became a wealthy man. Later he became a partner in computer company with four other people, which he now owns.

The first thing he did when he got money, he bought a big house for his mother, Margaret. Since that day until now, he spends his Sundays or holdidays at his mother's house for lunch with his sibling and her husband. Also, he bought an apartment for his sister and paid his brother's tuition, since he starts studying in a university and sleeping in a dorm.

"When will you join us" Jessica said to William when she came to see him "instead of sitting here alone."

"I am not alone. I am watching television."

"Okay can you join us, please?"

"As soon as I will get the beers I will join you."

Jessica left while William stayed in his place waiting for Ishtar

"I feel bored .... I wish William is with us." Julia said to Jessica while her eyes were on William

"Do not worry ....he is going to join us soon."

Ishtar came back with the bottles of beers. As soon as William saw her, he stood up opposite Ishtar and said "I can carry the bottles." William held the bottles

"Wait, wait." Ishtar said while William was still holding the tray. They gazed for seconds Ishtar seemed angry "What is the matter?" William asked

"Do you want to take them or not?" Ishtar said sharply

"No." William released the tray

Ishtar sighed then she asked "Where can i leave them?"

"To the game room." William replied

"Okay." Ishtar said then she turned her face from him

"Wait I will take mine." William said then he took one bottle of beer and left the rest

Ishtar looked at him in disbeliefing "I did not like what you did."

"This is my bottle." William said then he drank from his beer then he added while he was looking at Ishtar "I am thirsty."

"You can drink water."

"I want beer and I am paying for them."

Ishtar raised her eyebrows and said herself "He is so rude."

"Are you going to stay here?" William asked Ishtar when he started walking while Ishtar did not move. Ishtar looked at him then she walked beside him "Well, I thought you will change your mind."

"No I did not but you will get very good tip." William drank from his beer while Ishtar looked at the bottle which it is almost empty and said "You should drink water instead."

William looked at his bottle and said "No, I will just drink another one." Then they stopped when they stood beside Jessica

"Thank you." William said to Ishtar while he was holding the tray while Ishtar said nothing and turned her face away from him

"I need another beer, please." William said while Ishtar looked at him and said "Okay, I will bring more."

"You should come earlier instead of chatting with the waitress." Jessica said

"Why should I come earlier?"

"Because we are waiting you."

"You can play without me."

"We come together so we play together."

"I do not want to play and I do not like your rules."

"Can you play please?" Julia said

At that time Ishtar came back with a beer. William looked smiling at her and he walked toward her and held the bottle "Thanks."

"Anything else." Ishtar asked

"Five more minutes can i get more beer please?"

"Yes, sure." Ishtar said then she walked far from them "I guess tonight will be very long night." Ishtar said herself

"I am going back to my place." William said

"Why?" Julia asked

"I do not want to play." William said while he was walking

"I am coming with you." Julia walked with him while Jessica looked disappointed at her

"Okay." William said then they walked together

"What is your plan for tonight?" Julia asked

"I am going back to my apartment."

"Will you be alone?"

"Yes."

"Do you need company?"

William looked at his empty bottle then he looked around "I believe you can join me."

Julia seemed happy "Good."

Julia and Jessica are best friend since high school and William knows Julia since that time. First time William met Julia was at his mother's house during Jessica's prom then he started seen Julia regulary at Jessica's birthday or during her visit to Jessica. Since that time they become friends

"I did not like the place." Jessica said after they returned back to thier table

"Why?" Julia said

"Because no one agreed to play with her." Wiliam said

"This is not truth." Jessica said while she was looking at her brother "i just did not like the place." She added

"Any time you want to leave the bar the driver is ready to drive you home." William said

"Okay, we can stay longer." Jessica said

"I am going to stay with William." Julia said

"Okay good." Jessica said happily then she added "but before I leave I want to eat."

"I am going to order food." William said then he asked Ishtar for food and drink. After more than an hour Jessica and her fiancé left the bar alone while William and Julia stayed together in the bar

"How long are we going to stay here?" Julia asked while she was holding William left shoulder

"Soon." William said then he drank his beer and asked Ishtar for the bill. After fifteen minutes William and Julia left the bar while Ishtar was very disappointed

"What happened?" Maria asked Ishtar when she noticed Ishtar's sad face while they were in the kitchen room of the bar

"I can not believe he gave me one dollar tip …….. The whole night I was serving them!!!……" Ishtar sighed and said sadly

"Who are you talking about?!"

"A cusmoter and his girlfriend." Ishtar said

"Well, you have to expect every thing from people."

"But not a dollar."

"Some gave you a good tip other not. You will get good tips from others."

"If I see him again here, I am not going to serve him."

"Okay I will serve him."

"I should ignore him from beginning."

"You can not ignore a customer."

"He was rude from beginning."

"Maybe he did not have enough cash."

"He could get from his girl."

"Maybe they were drank."

Ishtar looked at her in disbelieve "why are you taking his side?"

"I am not taking his side." Maria said

"Yes, you are." Ishtar seemed unhappy

Maria sighed then she looked at her "Can you stop thinking about him and go back to work, please?"

"I will always remember him." Ishtar was angry

"Go back to work." Maria said then she walked away from Ishtar, whom said "He was rude and cheap." Then she followed Maria and got out of the kitchen room

On the next day William woke up late. He does not remember everything happened last night. But he knew he spent his night with Julia. He wore his shirt then left his room. After washing his face and brushing his teeth, he went to the kitchen. He was surprised when he saw Julia "I did not know you are here."

Julia was wearing his shirt alone without a bra. She smiled then she walked toward him "good morning, breakfast is ready" she said happily while she was touching his face

William pulled a chair then sat "I thought you left."

Julia pulled a chair for her and sat opposite William "You were sleeping…. I did not want to wake you up." Julia said with a smile

"Why will you wake me up?" William seemed unhappy

"To say goodbye." Julia said after seconds of thinking then she put her hand on William's left hand and smiled while William withdrew his hand then he sighed and asked her "When do you want to leave?"

Julia said sadly "I thought you want to spend your day with me"

"I have other thing to do."

"We can stay together for few hours."

William stood up and said "I am watching television. If you want any thing you will find me there."

"You do not want to eat your breakfast."

"I am not hungry." He said while he was leaving the kitchen room.

Julia did not want to leave, without spending some time with him. She looked at the breakfast that she made and felt sad then she threw it in the garbage. She collected the dishes and cleaned them then she left the kitchen room and walked toward William. She looked at William smiling while she was opening her shirt's buttons. She bent over him and started kissing his neck, his lips then his chest while William was trying to prevent her, but he could not. Finally he gave up.

She held his hand and said "shall we go to the bed." William said nothing while Julia led him to the room. William was not interesting in making any relationship with Julia and he told her before but Julia ignored what he said and started flirting and alluring him. Because he knew her for so long and she is his sister best friend did not want to hurt her and tried to be polite with her as a result he did not stop her and enjoyed his time with her.

Later in the evening of that day William went to bar which Ishtar works. He went alone without telling anyone.

When he saw Ishtar, he remembered her and asked her to serve him, but she ignored him and made herself busy. William did not like her attitude and waited for her to pass again from his side so he can ask her.

"She was very sweet and normal yesterday when I saw her although i was rude with her." William said himself when he was waiting for her to pass by his side

"Excuse me." William said but Ishtar ignored him again William tried to get her attention after she ignored her for awhile "There is something on your skirt."

"What?" Ishtar stopped and looked back at William.

"There is something on your skirt" William repeated

Ishtar asked "Where?"

"In the back of your skirt"

Ishtar moved close to him and looked confused on her skirt "Where?"

"In the back."

Ishtar turned her back skirt to the front and looked at it "Where? I can not see it." She said then she looked at William and saw him smiling

"There was nothing on your skirt, i was wrong."

"Really!"

"You have been ignoring me for no reason and i tried to get your attention."

"I believe you should be polite with me."

William sighed then he remembered his attitude when he was here yesterday and said "Can I get beer, please?"

Ishtar said after seconds of silent "I am busy now."

"I can wait, but my patient has limit. Stop behaving badly, I can tell to your manager, whom will dismiss you." William warned her

Ishtar looked disappointed and did not know what to say "I did not do any thing wrong …." She said in the end

"Oh, yah. You just make your customer unhappy." He explained

"Some one else can serve you … and …. I did not know that you are upset." Ishtar seemed unhappy

"Really."

Ishtar remembered when Maria told her about treating the customers nicely "okay, i will bring your order if you still want it." She said with a smile

William did not want their conversation to end, even though it was arguing. There was somthing pulled him toward her. Something he could not prevent it.

William looked at Ishtar, whom was waiting for his answer

"I need beer please." He said while Ishtar was unhappy and walked away from him while William was looking at her and smiling. In his second bottle of beer William asked for food while Ishtar just wrote on a paper without talking or looking at him.

After one hour William said himself "I do not why i keep looking at her. I should leave this bar instead of looking at her." then he called for Ishtar "Can I get the bill, please?"

"Yea, sure." Ishtar's face was still disappointed

After few minutes Ishtar gave the bill to William, she went back to his table to get the money. William was already left

"I guess tonight two dollars is his the tip." Ishtar said while she was getting William's bill. She held and walked back to the kitchen "wow i can not believe he did that." She was surprise and walked toward Maria, who was holding empty plates in her hands

"Do you remember I told you about a customer whom gave me a small amount of tip?"Ishtar asked Maria

Maria looked at her "Yes, I do."

"Tonight, the same person gave me ten dollars tip although he was alone."

Maria set the plates on empty table then she looked at Ishtar "You were wrong about him. I knew that."

"Yea, I was. I did not think he will give that much especially I behaved badly with him. Then he warned me....." Ishtar was talking very fast.

"He warned you." Maria seem angry

"Yes." Ishtar said sadly

"I told you to be patient and nice with everyone here and you can tell anyone if you need help."

"I know you did, but....." Ishtar could not find words

"But you judged him and ignored him." Ishtar did not say a word while Maria added "Maybe he does not have extra money."

"But I served him and his friends the whole night"

"And he gave you enough tonight."

"Maybe."

"Do not be greedy."

"I am not. I just need money and I deserve it." Ishtar said firmly

Maria looked at her "I am going back to my work."

"Okay, I am following you." Ishtar said then she followed Maria

—⟪⟫—

On Sunday was Jessica's birthday. Every member of her family gathered in her parents' house including Julia, whom was looking for William. As soon as she saw William, she followed him and stood beside him.

When Jessica blew the candles of her birthday's cake, William's cell phone started ringing. He looked at it then he walked away from them while Julia kept following him in her eyes then walked slowly behind him. She waited until he done from his call

"I was knocking at you door last night but you did not respond."

"Why do you want to see me?"

"I wanted to spend my night with you." Julia said happily

"I was not in my apartment."

"Where did you spend your night?" Julia was curious and afraid

"Away from my apartment." William was unhappy

Julia got closed to him "I just want to spend my night with you. You do not have to get angry."

William looked at her and said "I am not angry."

"Did you change your cell phone's number because I called you last night and there was no answer?" Julia said to William

"Who gave you my cell phone's number?" William said angry

"Is that matter?"

"Yes, it does."

"You have to know l care about you and I think about you all the time." Julia sighed

William looked at her silently. He heard these words from her before so Julia's confession did not change him, but he does not want to hurt her. He knows her from long time; moreover she is Jessica's best friend.

"I told you I do not have feeling for you and I will tell again I do not have feeling for you even after sleeping with you." William whispered

Julia smiled "I know you told but later your feeling will change about me."

"Maybe not."

"I belive I can change you."

"You will change me!" William was surprise

"Why can not I change you?"

"Because a woman can not change a man, unless he changes by himself."

"I am patient woman and I believe in myself."

"And I know myself very well."

"You care about me."

"You are my sister's best friend."

"Only because of that."

"Yes and sorry." William said while Julia seemed sad then she smiled and said "I do not care I believe you will change." William sighed and did not respond while Julia held his hand and looked happily at him while William seemed unhappy

"Sorry for interruption." William's mother Margaret said when she was standing behind them and carrying her puppy in her hands.

William turned at his mother and released his hand from Julia's hand while he was breathing a sigh of relief "Yes, mother." He said

"Do you want to eat a cake?" she asked them

William looked delightful when he saw his mother. She was a rescuer. He really did not know what to do with Julia "Yes, I want." He said then he started walking away from them

"I also want a cake." Julia said then she walked alone and sat beside Jessica then she started eating a cake and talking to her while William took his cake and got out of the room and started watching television.

"How is every thing?" Jessica asked

"Bad … bad." Julia said and her voice full of sadness

"Why? Tell me what happened?"

"Does he have a girlfriend?"

"No, he does not."

"Sure."

"Yes."

"So why is he not responding to me."

"Give him time Julia. He needs time"

Julia looked at William, whom was busy watching television "I know he needs time and I told him that." Julia stopped then she sighed

"What did he say?" Jessica asked

"He said he will not change."

"He will."

"I believe he will." Julia said then she smiled "I hope one day I will be apart from this family not a visitor as I am now."

Jessica looked at her "You are."

"I mean in different way." Julia said while she was looking happily at Jessica

"You will." Julia said then they looked at William "Everyone will be happy if you became his girlfriend."

"Then i come to this house with him."

Jessica looked at her "We can travel together or go on a double date."

"And spent our holidays in your mother's house."

"I am very excited for those thought."

"I am going to set beside him." Julia said then she stood up and walked toward William while Jessica kept looking at her.

On Friday Ishtar returned from work early but she did not find her mother and sister at home. She called her sister but she did not respond then she started baking some cookies. Later she sat on a couch and called her sister again but there was no answer. After few minutes the door opened and Ishtar's mother and her sister got into the house carrying bags in their hands. Ishtar ran to them and yelled on her sister "I was calling you why you did not answer."

"I was not able to respond." Ishtar's sister said then she went to the kitchen with the bags

"Why did you not respond?" Ishtar said while she was walking behind her

"I told you before, mother has a doctor's appointment." Ishtar's sister said

"I could not remember. You should remind me."

"And I thought you already know."

"How is every thing?"

"Every thing is perfect….. Her blood pressure, sugar and she lost few pound "

"This is good."

"Yea, it is." Ishtar's sister started to empty the bags "Why is too hot here?"

"I am baking."

Her sister seemed happy "What did you bake?"

"Some cooking and a cake."

Ishatr's sister started looking for cookies while Ishtar asked her "How many pounds did she lose?"

"Few." Ishtar's sister said then she held two cookies and walked toward Ishtar "When I was there with a doctor, I remembered last time when my mother had high blood pressure."

"You mean when we called the emergency."

"Yea, that time." Ishtar's sister said then she started eating the cookies

"I hope that will never happen again."

"If we keep watching her that will never happen again."

"I know." Ishtar said then she started checking the bag "What did you buy?" she asked

"Some fruit, vegetable and meat."

"Okay you will organize them. I am going to prepare for my second job."

Ishtar's sister said "But i do not want."

"I am leaving soon."

"Okay, fine." Ishtar's sister said while Ishtar left the kitchen room.

After more than half an hour, Ishtar left the apartment and got into Maria's car

"You seemed happy." Maria said when she started driving

"Yea, I am excited."

"Why?"

"I am not tired."

"Okay, this is good."

After few minutes Ishtar said "I wish i will see the man that I saw last week."

"Which man?"

"The man, who was rude to me."

"Who gave you one dollar tip?"

"Yes."

"You said he was rude with you."

"Yes, and I will argue with him if he does something bad." Ishtar said then they got out of the car

"You have to ignore him." Maria said while Ishtar said nothing

After hours of working Ishtar was bored and tired, she searched for William everywhere in the bar, but she could not find him. She was disappointed.

"Are you okay?" Maria asked her while they were getting an order in the kitchen

"Yes, i am.'

"You seemed unhappy."

"I am just tired."

"We will finish soon."

Ishtar sighed then she asked "By the way when is your doctor appointment?"

"It was last week."

"What did she say?"

"I did pregnancy test and it was negative."

"I am sorry." Ishtar felt bad

Maria looked at her and smile "we will keep trying." then she got the order and got out of the kitchen while Ishtar smiled and followed her with the order

—ɯ—

On Sunday afternoon, William returned to his apartment after he spent days out of city for business work. He was drinking a coffee when his door bell rang. As soon as he opened the door Jessica entered his apartment while William closed the door and followed her.

"Where have you been? I was worried about you. Julia and I called you several times but you did not respond."

"I am fine." William said then he asked her "Do you want coffee?"

"Did you hear what I said?" Jessica asked

"You were yelling but I understood." William said

"Julia came here and waited in front of your apartment's door." Jessica said while she was sitting on a chair.

"Why did she come?" William seemed unhappy then he strated walking toward the kitchen.

"She cares about you." Jessica said while she was walking behind him

"I was busy." William said while he was adding more coffee to his cup while Jessica made one for her "what did you do in the last days?" Jessica asked while they were returning back to the living room

"I was working."

"You did not have five minutes extra to respond to my call." Jessica seemed sad

"I forgot my cell phone here." He sat on a sofa

Jessica put her coffee on a table "this coffee is so sweet."

"There is more coffee if you want."

"No I do not want." Jessica looked around and saw some clothes on a couch and looked at dusty table. She stood up while she was saying "By the way your apartment is so messy."

"I was busy and I am tired."

"I will tell my mother to send her house keepers here to clean it. Now gave me the key before I leave so I can make copy of it." Jessica moved toward William and opened her left hand.

"There is no key. Did you forget what you did last time when I gave you the key?" William looked at Jessica's eyes while Jessica tried to ignore him. He waited for Jessica to respond but she did not she only was smiled.

"Do you remember?" William asked again

"Yes, I do."

William drank from his coffee then he looked around and said "please tell my mother to send some one to clean the house."

"Yes I will and give me the key, so I can give it to my mother."

"No, there is no key." William insisted

"Okay I understood." Jessica said while she was raising her right hands

"Did you think I am stupid to give you my key? William said while Jessica was turning toward the door to leave then she looked at him and smiled "No, you are not."

Then they walked together to the door and William watched her until she disapper then he said himself when he was locking the apartment door "She wants the kye so she can give it to her friend Julia."

Few years ago, William made a copy of his apartment's key to his mother so she can send someone to clean it when he is away. But Jessica took the key and gave it to William's girlfriend, who was already broke up with her. In morning when he woke up he found her in his apartment. Since then William changed his key and he never gave it again to his sister and told his mother what Jessica did.

At night William was drinking, when heard knocking on the door. He wondered who will visit him at this time. He looked at a peephole door, but no body was there. He stayed in his spot and waited few seconds to make sure he heard the knocking. After few seconds there was a knocking again.

When he opened the door, he was totally surprised "Julia … what are you doing here??"

"I come to see you."

"I am so tired."

"Are you alone?"

"Yes." the word yes encourage Julia to spend her night with him. She entered his apartment without his permission

"I missed you." She said smoothly.

William sighed then said "What do you want?"

"Nothing. I just want to spend my night with you." She moved close to him smiling

"I want to be alone, please." William said

Julia looked at his galss of drink that William was holding in his right hand and said "Can I drink first then I will leave." Then she grabbed his glass of drink from his hand and moved inside his apartment. William sighed then he closed the door and followed her.

"I called you many times." she said while she was sitting on a chair.

"I knew …. Jessica told me." He said while he was grabbing a glass that was beside the liqure rock. He filled his glass with a drink then he walked toward Julia. Then he noticed she took her jacket off and her dress exposed her body. She was wearing a black short dress with deep v neck

"Where had you been gone in the past days?" she asked him after he sat beside her

"I was out of city."

"Alone."

"No, I was with business men."

"Any one else." she was curious

"No, only us."

"Did you go somewhere else?"

"Why are you asking me those questions?" William seemed unhappy

"I just want to know."

"Know what?"

"Who was with you?"

William sighed then he asked after seconds of silent "when are you going to leave?"

"What?" Julia was surprise

"I am tired and I want to sleep."

Julia moved closed to him then she sat on his lap "but I do not want to leave."

"I want to sleep." William said

"We can sleep together." Julia said then she started kissing him

"I said I am tired."

"You can relax in the room." Julia said then she kissed his lips. She held his hand then stood up. She walked to his bedroom while she was holding his right hand

———m———

On Wednesday night, Ishtar did not sleep well. She woke up after midnight to go to the washroom, and when she was going back to her room, heard her mom was crying. She opened her mother's door room and asked "Are you okay?..... Mom … are you sick?" Ishtar was sad and terrified

"No I am not." She responded

Ishtar turned the light on and walked toward her mother, whom she was sitting on her bed. Ishtar sat beside her mother and asked her sweetly "Why are you crying?"

"I had a bad dream."

"What was about?"

"About you."

Ishtar looked at her "I am alright and setting beside you."

"You were returning from your night job and someone attacked you."

Ishtar looked sadly at her "Try to sleep again."

"You have to quit your night job."

"I will quit as soon as I find another job."

"If you are working because of me, I am fine. I will stop taking medicine."

"You have to take your medicine." Ishtar seemed disappointed

"But you have to quit."

"I will." Ishtar sighed then she added "Can you sleep again, please?"

"Yes, I will." Ishtar's mother layed on the bed while Ishtar was comforting her. After fifteen minutes Ishtar left the room after her mother stopped crying. She returned back to her room and tried to sleep but she could not, finally she slept before dawn. As a result in morning when she woke up, she was half an hour late from her shift. She did not make her coffee as usual. She washed her face and brushed her teeth as fast as she could and left the apartment immediately. She missed her first bus. Then after ten minutes of waiting at bus stop she got into another one. Unfortunatttly when she got of the bus, it was raining. She sought for her umbrella in her back bag but she could not find it. She walked in the rain for few minutes until she reached the library. Ishtar's hair and clothes were wet. She went to lunch room and took off her long jacket then she tried to dry her hair.

During her working time, Ishtar was coughing and sneezing .Those symptoms continued until she arrived home. As soon as she arrived home, she went immediately to her room while he mother followed her

"You look tired. Are you okay?" Ishtar's mother asked

"No, I feel cold." Ishtar sat on her bed and covered herself by a blanket

Her mother stood beside her "What happened to you."

"I walked in the rain."

His mother seemed sad "What do you want me to make for you?"

"Anything worm."

"Okay." Her mother said then left the room while Ishtar was shivering in her bed

"Drink this one. You will feel better." Her mother said when she came back and gave a cup of hot milk

Ishtar looked at the cup "Can I get a tea please instead of this milk?"

"Okay, sure."

"I need a pill also."

"There are no pills left; called your sister to buy medicine in her way home."

"Why there are no more pills?"

"I do not know. You can ask your sister when she came back." Her mothe said while she was leaving the room

Ishtar started shivering, and she has to wait her sister more than four hours until she will arrive home. She closed her eyes and said "Maria is at home. I will ask her if she can buy pills and bring them."

About a half an hour Maria was there with her puppy Bella, which she started barking when she saw Ishtar while Ishatr was smiling to her

"Did you check your temperature?" Maria asked

"Yes... It is normal now." Ishtar looked at Maria and said "Thank you for coming."

"You are my best friend." Maria said then she took Bella and put her beside Ishtar's feet. Maria lives in a house, which is near to Ishtar's apartment. She bought the house five years ago with her boyfriend. A year ago, they adopted Bella. She also tried to have a child, and now she has a treatment in order to get a child. From time to time Ishtar visited Maria in her house.

"Did you bring medicine?"

"Yes, I did." Maria said while she was giving it to her then she added "I am going to bring water."

"Okay." Ishtar said while Maria was leaving the room and left her puppy on Ishtar's bed. Ishtar looked smiling at the puppy. Then after a minute Maria came back with bottle of water

"I told you several times to find a boy friend." Maria said to Ishtar while she was giving her water

"What?" Ishtar was surprise

"Of course if you have a boyfriend, you would not be suffering." Ishtar did not respond while Maria countiued "Maybe he could buy you a car or drop you at your work, instead of walking under the rain." Maria said while Ishtar was taking the medicine

"I believe the right word is a bank account." Ishtar said while Maria looked at her then Ishtar added "I can do every thing by myself and if I have enough money I would not be walking under the rain."

Maria looked in disbelieve "everyone needs help. Everyone needs someone can help them."

"I do not need any one."

"Oh, yea, you did not even have a medicine."

"I need a medicine not someone."

"Someone will take care of you."

"I can do by myself."

"I know you can but sometime we need help."

Maria cares about Ishtar, and tried before to match her with some men she knows, but Ishtar always said there is no chemistry or knowing them about her virginity; it will change their concepts about dating her.

"So you will always be a virgin." Maria said after minutes of silent

"I will be a virgin until the day of my wedding."

"You will change your mind when you will meet someone like my boyfreind." Then she added with a smile "You will sleep with him from first date." Ishtar looked unhappy at her

"If a man loves me, he is going to understand and respect every thing about me."

"Some of them do not want a virgin woman."

"This will be a gift for him."

"A gift! He does not want it."

"I do not want him either or care about his opinion or even want to date him." Ishtar was angry. She took a deep breath then she added "I prefer to stay pureness my whole life instead of loving a man, who only loves my body."

"If you keep saying that you will stay for the rest of your life virgin."

"I can not believe you still talking about my virginity." Ishtar was very disappointed

Maria looked at her "I am sorry. I care about you." Ishtar looked at her and smiled while Maria added "by the way living with someone without marriage is great."

"Maybe."

"You are wrong and one day you will change your mind when you find the right person."

"Maybe."

"I believe it will happen." Maria said while Ishtar did not respond "I will leave you now to relax." Maria stood up and carried her dog

"Okay, I will try to sleep." Ishtar said

"I will come back later." Maria said while Ishtar nodded her head and smiled while Maria added warmly "take care of yourself." Then she left the room while Ishtar lay down in her bed

On Friday night, Ishtar was busy with the people in the bar, when she noticed William entered the bar. She looked at him and said herself "I have not seen him for days. I thought he is not coming here anymore." Then William passed by her and smiled while Ishtar smiled back to the mystery man. She felt excited to see him again there. She finished her order then she walked towords him. He was sitting beside the window in one of the bar's corner

"Hello." Ishtar said happily when she stood in front of William

William looked at her then he said while he was smiling "hello."

"You have not been here for a while." Ishtar could not believe what she said to him

William looked at her in disbelief. "I was busy."

Ishtar looked disappointed and kept silent for second then she asked him "How can I help you?"

William said "As usual I want beer."

Ishtar walked as fast as she can while William kept looking through the window again

"I can not believe what I did." She said herself while was getting beer. She stopped for seconds in her sopt then she took a deep breath

"Are you okay?" Maria, who was behind her, asked

Ishtar looked at her "Yes, I am."

"It does not seem you are okay." Ishtar did not respond while Maria asked "Do you still sick?"

"The customer that I told you about him is here."

"Did he bother you?"

"No."

"If anyone bothers you let me know."

Ishtar smiled "Sure."

"I am going back to my customer." Maria said then she walked far from Ishtar while

Ishtar nodded her head and got out of the kitchen with a bottle of beer. In her way back to William, she said her self while she was looking at him "He does not look as always. He seemed distracted and careless." Ishtar kept looking at him while holding a bottle of beer in her hand. She set the bottle on a table with smile while William just thanked her without even looking at her

"I was right something is going on with him." Ishtar said herself while she was walking further from William. She stopped infront of staff enters and looked at William

"What are you doing here go back to your work?" A deep voice behind her ordered

Ishtar looked at person who is behind her. it was Maria's voice "Do you like my voice?"

"No." Ishtar was angry

"Who is he?" Maria asked while she moving Ishtar from her way. She looked at the place that Ishtar was looking and asked "Is he attractive?"

"Nobody ...." Before Ishtar completed her sentence Maria asked "who is he?"

Ishtar opened her mouth to say somthing, but Maria started guessing "he is not that one, who is sitting with a girl. And he is not part of a group because they seemed all of them are couples." Maria looked at Ishtar, whom seemed disappointed while Maria said "Oh I know who he is." Maria looked back again at the place where William was sitting and said "he is the one who is sitting alone and looking outside."

"Instead of gossiping about people, go and take the customers order." One of their co-workers said

They looked at him both of them. He was angry. They looked at each other then they walked in different direction. After less than fifteen minutes William asked for another drink while Ishtar smiled and walked as fast as she could to get beer for William

"Are you okay?" Ishtar asked William when she set his bottle of drink in a table

"Yes, I am." William was surprised then he smiled "Thanks for asking."

"Do you need anything?" Ishtar seemed concern

"No, thank you." William replied without looking at her while Ishtar kept looking at him

"You can leave." William said to Ishtar, whom seemed very distracted. She walked slowly while William held his cell phone. Ishtar ran into the washroom. She opened the door and slammed. She took a deep breathe and looked at the mirror "I am very stupid and annoying girl." She was angry on herself. She took a deep breathe again "Why did

I ask him questions I do not know even his name?" she inhaled then she got out of the washroom.

"He is a handsome man" Maria whispered in Ishtar's left ear when they were in a kitchen room

"Who?" Ishtar seemed annoyed

"The man, who you were looking at, he seems good."

"Please, Maria I am in bad mood." Ishtar begged Maria

"Are you okay?" Maria seemed concern

"Yes I am." Ishtar smiled then she held a plate of chicken wings and prepared to get out of the kitchen

"He is alone, right?" Maria asked

Ishtar looked at her and explained "He is the same customer that I told you about before."

Maria raised her eyebrow and said "Oh, so you know him."

"Yes." Ishtar said then she walked away from Maria "I can not wait to go home." Ishtar said herself when she got out of the kitchen then she went to her customers and gave them the order then William asked her for bill. At this time Ishtar did not care about the amount of tip

On Sunday, it was rainy and cold day. Ishtar, her mother and sister decided to go shopping and buy clothes for their mother. After seeing few stores their mother seemed bored and disappointed because she did not see anything that she likes

"Down stairs there is a big store, we can see their clothes." Ishtar suggested to her mother. The store's prices are over her budget but she wanted to make her mother happy

"I am tired and hungry." Her mother said

"We will eat after buying clothes."

They took an elevator to down stair and walked slowly to the store. At the front door of the shop's store. Ishtar and William saw each other. William was with a woman. He was holding bags in his hands and leaving the store, while Ishtar was entering the store. She was walking behind her sister and her mother. They gazed for seconds, and then they continue their own way.

"I am going washroom." Ishtar said after seconds of being inside the store. She walked as fast as she could and started searching for William

"I am so stupid." She said herself after two minutes of leaving her mother and sister alone. She shook her head and went back to them. After they bought a long black skirt for their mother they headed to the food court to eat.

"I need some medicine." Ishtar's mother announced

"We will buy them on our way home." Ishtar said

"Are we going home immediately after leaving the mall?"

"I want to go home." Ishtar said

"Yes we will." Ishtar's sister said

After finishing shopping, William and his mother, who was shopping with him, went home. Margaret, who is William's mother, she is fifty five years old. She was in high school, when she became a pregnant. Her boyfriend, who was one year older than her, left her when he knew she was a pregnant. When William born, Margaret left school and started raising him. She lived in small apartments for period time then she moved to a basements. She lived in different places and moved many times. At the same time she was working as a baby sitter. When William went to school, Margaret met his teacher. They started dating for years later they got married and they still together until now. They have two children, Jessica and Martin.

"When will I meet your girlfriend?" Margaret asked William when they were eating their lunch in his mother's house

"There is no girlfriend."

"I thought Julia is your girlfriend, is she not?"

"No, she is not." William was angry then he added "she is only just a friend."

His mother looked at him "Just a friend."

William hoped his mother to stop talking about Julia "Only a friend."

"Really!" his mother disbelief him

William knows his mother. She will never stop asking him questions until he tells her the truth especially his mother is very eager to meet a woman calls his girlfriend "we are not dating." William said

His mother sighed then said sadly "I do not know when you will settle."

"I will settle when you stop asking me the same question over and over again." William was disappointed

His mother looked at him and asked him when he was standing "Where are you going?"

"I need some water." William walked to the fridge

"When you travel next time tell me, please?"

"Why?" he asked when he was sitting again beside her

"I have to know." William smiled and nodded his head while his mother added "tomorrow I will send someone to clean your apartment?"

"My apartment is clean." William said while his mother looked at him and added "in the afternoon someone will be there." William said nothing

At night William left his mom's house and decided to go to the bar, where Ishtar works. He was sitting alone, When Maria saw him. She walked straight toward him and asked "May I help you?"

William hesitated before saying ".... I am waiting a friend."

He lied. There was no friend, but he wanted to see Ishtar.

He was looking right, left and everywhere, but she did not appear. He waited more than fifteen minutes for Ishtar to come from somewhere but that did not happen. Finally he gave up and called Maria "I think my friend is not coming, so can I get a bottle of beer."

"Any thing else." Maria asked after he said to her the name of his favourite beer.

"No thanks." William replied

William was drinking his beer, but his eyes were searching again for Ishtar. He sighed twice and started playing in his cell phone, so the time will pass quickly.

He waited another fifteen minutes then asked Maria "There is a women, works here has a long ....". Before William completed his sentence, Maria knew the women, who William was asking for. "I think you are asking about Ishtar. She is not working tonight."

"Why? Is she sick?" William asked anxiously.

"No, she is not. She does not work Sundays. Only on Fridays and Saturdays she works."

William was disappointed then he said "Oh okay and thank you."

Maria smiled then she asked "Do you want to leave her a message? I am her best friend."

William did not know what to say. He was surprised by Maria's question. "No...... nothing. Mostly i see her when i come here, so I am asking you about her."

After five minutes William left the bar, but another surprise was waiting him when he reached his apartment. Julia was there waiting him.

"I have been waiting here for a while. I missed you." She put her arms around William's neck.

William released his neck from her arms and asked "What do you want?"

"Let's talk inside." She pointed toward his apartment.

"You have to leave. I am already tired and in bad mood." William said firmly while Julia was very disappointed

"Why? What happened?"

"Nothing. "

"You know I have feeling for you, right?" She said sweetly.

"Yea, I know. Thanks for your feeling but......" before William added a word Julia said while her hand was on his lips "I did not ask you for anything."

"I am sorry...."

"I know you are in a bad mood so I will leave."

William looked at her and remembered she is his sister's best friend "You can come in."

Julia looked in disbelief at him "You change your mind."

William smiled then opened his apartment's door and entered "Do you want to come in?"

"Yes." Julia said happily then she got into the apartment

"Do you want a drink?" William asked her while they were walking inside the apartment

"Yes." Julia said then she sat on a couch

"Vodka!" William asked while he was standing beside the liqure rock

"Yes, please."

William got the bottle of vodka and poured in two glasses while Julia said herself while she was looking lovely and happily at him "Soon I will be your girlfriend."

31

At the same night Ishtar could not sleep because she woke up late in the morning. She tried to sleep on her back and on her stomach but she could not. Then she started flipping on her left and right side to sleep but she could not

"Stop making noise." Her sister commanded when she was covering her face "I want to sleep."

"I can not sleep."

"Do not make noise; please just leave the room."

Ishtar sighed and covered her face in trying to sleep. After few minutes Ishtar unveiled her face and whispered "did you sleep?"

"I am trying to sleep but you are not letting me." Her sister was angry

"By the way, what did the man give you?" Ishtar asked after few seconds of silent

The question surprise her sister "Which man?"

"Pharmacist, I saw him giving you a paper when I was waiting outside with my mom."

Her sister did not respond while Ishtar said "I am still waiting."

"I can not remember what he gave me."

"I know you are lying." Ishtar said after few minutes of silent

"He gave me his cell phone's numbers."

"What?" Ishtar was surprised and raised her head

"Yea." Her sister said happily

"Tell me the whole story." Ishtar sat on the bed and turned the lamp that was on her night table on

Her sister nodded her head and said happily "a month ago, I noticed, he was looking at me secretly when i was with my mother taking the medicine, but I ignored him. Recently I started missing him …. I want to see him …. Talk to him …"

"What happened later?" Ishtar was curious

"He always flirts with me."

"What did he say?"

"He tells me how gorgeous i am and my smile is most beautiful smile in the world." Ishtar's sister was talking while touching her hair by her left hand

"This is sweet." Ishtar said with smile

"Yes, so when he gave me his call phone's number i could not refuse."

"Did you call him?"

"No, not yet."

"Why?"

"I do not know."

"Does he have your cell phone number or not?"

"No, I did not."

"You can give him your phone number."

"I am waiting to see him again."

"When?"

"Tomorrow."

"But you picked mother's medicine today."

"I know."

"What are you going to tell him?"

"I will tell him I want to see him."

"You do not want to call him but you want to see him."

"Seen him is so different."

"How?"

"I can see his reaction and his emotions when i talk to him." Ishtar seemed surprise while her sister said "If he asks me for a date I will go."

"You did not give him your phone number and now you decide to go on date with him."

"There is more benefit on being in date than talking on a phone."

"How?"

"I will get free food."

Ishtar looked at her in disbelief "I am not surprise."

"I love food."

Ishtar layed down in her bed and turned the light off "Good night."

"Good night." Her sister said then she layed down in her bed

Chapter Two

FIRST DATE

On Friday night, Ishtar and Maria were in their way to their job at the bar. "If I ask you to work on Sunday, will you accept?" Maria asked Ishtar.

"No, on Monday I have to get up early for my job in library." Ishtar looked at her and asked "Why are you asking?"

"There was one person wanted to see you last Sunday."

"Who?"

"Can you guess?"

"You are the only person that I know."

"Anothe person."

"Your boyfriend."

Maria looked in disbelief at her "You only know me and my boyfriend in this whole city."

Ishtar begged Maria "Please, tell me who the person is?"

"The man, who was sitting alone, and you were looking at him." Maria said happily

Ishter felt happy when she heard that. She pointed at herself and smiled then she said "He asked you ……. About me ….."

"Yes, he did." Maria looked at her and added "Purposely I told you today, so I see your reaction."

Ishtar looked at Maria and asked "Did you see my sister recently?"

"No, why?"

"She was talking about reaction same as you."

"Because we are right." Maria said while Ishtar said nothing

After seconds of silent Maria looked at Ishtar and said "I think you care about him."

"No….. I don't…" Ishtar said so fast

"Yes you do." Maria was surprise

"Last time when i saw him I tried to talk to him he did not seem interest."

"You talk to him about what?" Maria was surprise

"I asked him why he was away for a while."

"Some men do not like chat about blah blah blah."

"What does that mean?"

"Maybe he has boring day."

"What does men like?" Ishtar asked after seconds of thought

"Being in date with very attractive woman and having free sex."

"What does free sex mean?"

"Having casual relationship or skipping dates."

"Oh."

"My last boyfriend was like that." Maria said then she said "So you care about the mystery man."

After seconds of thinking Ishtar looked at Maria and said "maybe."

"I was right."

"I said maybe."

Maria looked at her and said "I admire you." Ishtar looked confused at her while Maria added "you can control your emotions."

"What?" Ishtar saw surprised

"You are tough woman." Ishtar said nothing while Maria said "you have not been in love, have you?"

"In love, no." Ishtar said immeditally

Maria looked at her and said "I was right." Ishtar looked at her and said nothing.

"You are my best friend." Maria said after minutes of silent "Always remember I love you. I said that because I care about you."

Ishtar looked at her "Sometimes I hate you."

"I know." Maria smiled then she added "Sometimes I say stupid things to you." Ishtar looked at her smiling and noding her head while Maria said kindly "I am sorry."

"By the way I am not dying."

"Did I mention death?" Maria was angry

"So stop apologizing." Ishtar said wormly while Maria smiled

As soon as they arrived, Ishtar wore her clothes faster than other times. She hoped to see the mystery man, who asked about her. The bar was so romantic. It was dark and illuminated by candles and that hinders Ishtar from seeing William.

"Why is the bar like that?" Ishtar asked Maria

"What do you mean by like that?"

"The bar is dark and I can not see clearly."

"Are you blind?......It will be always like that." Maria looked at her and shook her head in disbelief "ofcourse you do not like something romantic."

"People are coming here to eat not to live a love story."

"Candles with food make them eat more."

"Oh yea let bring my sister here and she will be the judge."

"You sister is not romantic."

"And everyone here is romantic."

"Yes."

"Even men who is looking for casual relationship."

Maria looked angry at her "I do not know. You can ask the manger why we have candles in the bar."

"I almost fell down."

Maria sighed and said "Be careful when you walk."

"I barely can see."

The darkness prevented Ishtar from recognizing people. She wanted to see William. She looked at his spot where he always sits, but the place was empty.

"Is the handsome man here?" Maria asked Ishtar while they were getting the order for customers

"Who?"

"The man who asked me about you?"

"Well, I can not see him because of the darkness."

"If I see him, I will let you know."

"It does not matter."

"You have to know."

"Maybe, I am his favorite waitress."

"Maybe." Maria said while Ishtar walked with the order far from her

After an hour, William was there. He was alone but this time he sat in a different place, which was in a corner and in front of him there was a small table. He sought for Ishtar, especially he knows tonight she is working there. When he found her, his eyes followed her every movement while his left hand was on the table and the right hand was holding his chin. He waited for her, but she did not pass in front of him. When he got tired from waiting, he ordered a drink.

After an hour William left the bar. Later he regretted of coming early home and decided to stay longer next time.

Ishtar was disappointed and tired when she finished her job. On their way home she was mostly silent and replying Maria's question with anger.

"Can I know what is going on with you?" Maria was worry

"Nothing, I have a headache."

"Did you see the man, who asked about you?" Maria seemed excited

Ishtar sighed "I can not even remember his face."

Maria looked her at in disbelief "Oh really."

"Do you think if he was there, I could see him?"

"You have to use to the candles. We mostly have them."

"Will we have the light tomorrow?"

"Yes." Maria said while Ishtar sighed and did not respond

The next day William went again to the bar. He sat alone in the same place that he used to sit, beside the window. He sat purposely there, hoping to see Ishtar. After few minutes Ishtar saw him and walked slowly toward him

"Hello." Ishtar said with a smile

William smiled and looked at Ishtar's eyes directly and said "How are you?"

"Good, Thanks."

"I am glad to see you." William said with a smile while Ishtar smiled and did not say a word. "I do not like this spot….. can I move to another table. " William said while he was pointing at the place where he wants to move in. "If you do not mind, can you bring my drink there." William said kindly

Ishtar looked at the place that William pointed and seemed careless "Yes, of course."

"Thanks."

Ishtar moved quikly far from him while William moved to the new spot "I guess he forgot what he wanted to tell me on that day." Ishtar said herself while she was walking to get William order, who was watching her excitly.

Ishtar was setting a drink on the table, when William said "My name is William."

"Ishtar….. My name is Ishtar." she said her name and walked as fast as she could while William seemed happy

"Can I ask you question." William asked Ishtar after she brought another drink for him

"Sure."

"I know you do not work here tomorrow….. So do you have a plan … or are you available tomorrow?" William seemed nervous

"What do mean by plan?" Ishtar was curious

"I mean busy." William did not know how to invite Ishtar or ask her for a date. William was confused and hesitated in his words while Ishtar seemed confused and said nothing

"Can we go outside together…… for a cup of coffee … or for a walk…." William finally said

"No, I can not, my mother is sick and I want to be with her." Ishtar was surprised

"Oh. We can go another day." William was disappointed

Ishtar looked at him and felt bad "Sorry, I have to go back to work." She wanted to be with him while William said "Can I get the bill?"

Ishtar looked at him and said "Sure."

Ishtar walked slowly and sadly.

On thier way back to home, Maria asked Ishtar about William but Ishtar said to her that she did not see him during her shift.

On Sunday, while Ishtar was sweeping the floor when she heard knocking on a door. She left the broom on a floor and ran to the door

"Thanks for coming." Ishtar said to Maria, when she opened the door

"As soon as I saw your message, I came in." Maria got into the apartment "What do you want to tell me?"

"Do you want coffee?" Ishtar asked while she was closing the door

"Yes." Maria said then she asked while they were walking to the kitchen room "Are you alone?"

"Yes, I think they are in a church."

Ishtar made a cup of coffee for Maria. She sighed and said while she was setting Maria's cup on a table infront of her "Yesterday I lied on you."

"About what?"

"The man, who was looking for me when i was not working." Ishtar stopped then she added "I saw him last night."

"And?" Maria seemed excited

"I think he asked me out."

"What?" Maria was surprise and stood up

"I refused." Ishtar sighed and sat on a chair beside Maria

"Refused! Why?" Maria, who was shock, said loudly

"I was afraid and panic."

"He is not a monster to be afraid." Maria looked confuse while Ishtar, who was sad, said nothing "Did he ask you to go home with him?" Maria asked

"No."

"So why you were afraid."

"I do not know."

"What did he say when you said you can not?"

"He said we can go next time." Ishtar looked at Maria and said "You think he will ask me again."

"Maybe." Maria raised her eyebrows and sipped from her coffee while she was sitting on her chair

"I think i will say yes if he ask me again." Ishtar said while she was holding her cup of coffee in her both hands.

Maria looked at her "Maybe he will not ask you again so you do not have to hold on for any thoughts or hope."

"You think he will not ask me again." Ishtar seemed disappointed

"You rejected him."

"I did not."

"Yes, you did." Maria stood up "You care about him but you refused him." Ishtar said nothing while Maria added "It is only eating food with someone for first time. This is the meaning for first date."

"I do not know what happened to me."

"Will you go on a date if he asks you again?"

"You think he will ask again?"

"I said maybe." Maria said while Ishtar seemed disappointed "What is his name?" Maria asked happily

"His name is William."

"What else he said?" Maria was curious

"Nothing."

"Okay I have to leave." Maria said then she stood up

"Where are you going?" Ishtar stood beside her

"I am going to buy pregnancy test."

"I hope you will be pregnant."

"Well, we will keep trying and I am waiting for the result." Maria said while she was getting out of the kitchen with Ishtar then Maria looked around the house and asked before getting out "Where is your Christmas tree?"

"I am always tired. I do not think I can set Christmas tree."

"I can help you with it." Maria smiled then she added "By the way I am spending Christmas out of city."

"What?"

"Yea, we need this vacatoion so we can keep trying to make babies."

Ishtar smiled "How long will you be away?"

"For ten days."

Ishtar seemed unhappy "What? Even New Years Eve you will not be here."

Maria looked at her "You have your mother and sister."

"I see them everyday."

"Find you a man."

"I told you, if he asks me again, I will accept his invitation."

"Then you can spend your New Year eve with him and lose your virginity."

"Only a date."

Maria opened the door of the apartment "I have to go now."

40

"Good luck." Ishtar said and crossed her fingers while Maria smiled and crossed her fingers also then she walked away while Ishtar smiled then she closed the apartment door

Christmas was coming and every one was busy. The bar got busy, and was lighted by candles. Ishtar looked exhausted. She was complaining about the bar and the weather. She did not see William for weeks and most of the time was distracted and sad

"Take a day off woman." Maria, who was raising her both hand in the air said to Ishtar when she heard her complaining about the bar.

"I do not want."

"So you shut up." Maria said madly and loudly

William was sitting with another man in different place, which it was higher than other places. He climbed two stairs before he sat at his place. Ishtar's face shone, when she saw him. It had been long time since she saw him or since she refused to go out with him. She walked happily toward them, but William looked unhappy when he saw her. He did not even smile when Ishtar asked him what they want for drinking.

He seemed so serious and Ishtar was disappointed. She turned her back and sighed. It is her fault and nobody else to blame for his reaction. She rejected him when he asked her out. And now he will never ask her out again. He had been gone for weeks and now he is looking at her as he does not know her. Ishtar was thinking in William's reaction when she was descending the two stairs. Ishtar stumbled when she was getting down the last stairs. Fortunately she did not fall down because William was holding her from her back. Then he got down the stairs and stood in front of her while Ishtar was standing on the second stair and looking unhappy at him.

"Are you okay?" William looked at her and asked "for moment i was afraid." he sighed while Ishtar could not respond and she was surprised by William's reaction "You look tired." William pointed on a chair next to them "Why do not you sit here?"

"I am okay." she got down the stairs and tried to walk away, but William prevented her by standing opposite her "You do not seem you are okay."

At that time Maria approached from them and asked "Everything is okay."

Ishtar opened her mouth and tried to say something, but William spoke before her "She is tired." he pointed on Ishtar

Maria looked at William and said "I knew but she is so stubborn." Then she looked at Ishtar and said "look at her, her hand is shaking," she looked at Ishtar's right hand, while Ishtar tried to hide it.

"I am fine." Ishtar was tring to prevent William's eyes.

"You almost fall down." William was calm and polite

"I told you to go home and take some rest, but you never listen." Maria said sadly

"I am able to work." She turned her face to walk away.

William said suddenly "I can drop you home…. If you want."

Ishtar stopped and looked behind her, but before saying a word Maria said angry "Go home," Maria walked toward Ishtar and blocked her way and whispered "Do not be stupid again."

Ishtar did not move or said any words "I am going to speak with the manager while you are changing your clothes." William suggested

"Okay, I will leave." Finally Ishtar agreed while William looked happy and Maria breathed a sigh of relief.

She changed her clothes as fast as she could and the smile on her face. Then she leaned on the wall and the smile still on her face and breathed a big sigh of happiness. Then took her purse and got out of the room.

William smiled when he saw her then they walked together and got out of the bar. He opened the door for her then he got into the car

"I am so glad you finally agreed with me." William said while he was looking at her

"Agree about what?"

"To leave the bar and have some rest."

"Yea, I need some rest." Ishtar said then she gave him the address of her apartment which it was not far the bar. They spent the first five minutes in silent then William looked at her and smiled, Ishtar also smiled. Later she turned her consideration to the outside, and then closed her eyes. William looked at her and asked kindly. "Do you feel better?"

"Yes, I am alright, but I will be better when I will sleep in my bed."
William smiled "how is your foot?"
"There is no pain now"
"This is good." Ishtar smiled and said nothing. After few minutes William said while he was looking at Ishtar "We arrived."
"Thank you." Ishtar said kindly
William got off the car and opened the door for her "I hope you will feel better."
"Thank you." Ishtar said happily
"Good night and sweet dreams." William said happily
"Good night." Ishtar said then she turned and walked slowly in her way while William kept watching her until she disappeared then he left. That night Ishtar was so excited and slept peacefully. She hoped William to ask her again out because this time she will agree.

Next day was Sunday, Ishtar woke up early. She was happy and feeling better. She woke up before her mother and started preparing to go to the church. Before they left the apartment, Ishtar left a note for her sister telling her where her mother and her are. The church was not far from their house, they took a bus to get into the church. On their way home, it was already at noon so they stopped on some stores to buy some food. When they arrived home, Ishtar's sister was awake and waiting for them.

"I wish every Sunday; I can attend Sunday mass like today." Ishtar's mother said when they sat to eat.
"You can pray at home. It is same thing." Ishtar said
"I prefer going to the church." Ishtar's mother said
Ishtar looked at her mother then she looked at her sister and said "she can take you there." Ishtar's sister, who was eating, looked surprise at her
"Why do I have to take her to the church?" Ishtar's sister asked
"Because I can not."
"You did today so you can do every Sunday."
"I did today because I woke up early." Ishtar was angry
"You can do the same thing every Sunday."
"I left my job early last night ....."
"Shut up both of you." Their mother yelled on them while both of them looked at her and said nothing then they started eating. After few minutes Ishtar's cell phone rang. She got up and took her cell phone

from her purse. She looked at it to see who is calling her but she did not regognize the number. She looked at her mother and her angry sister then she left the kitchen.

"Hello." Ishtar said while she was entering her room

"Hey, how are you?" a sweet voice asked

Ishtar could not recognize the voice. She sat on the edge of her bed and asked "Who is calling?"

"It is me..... William," Ishtar smiled and walked to the door and closed it while William added "I called to know how you feel today."

"I am fine ..... But how you got my phone's number?" Ishtar asked.

William smiled then he said "As you know it Christmas time, as a result I got it from Santa clues....," both smiled then William said kindly "I do not want to annoy you. I know you are tired..."

"No. I am fine," Ishtar said so fast because she did not want from William to end his call

"I am so happy to hear that."

"I was so stressed from my jobs and home." She explained

"Why? What happened?"

"Oh, just too much to do especially during this time."

"Did you sleep well last night?" William asked kindly

"Yes, I slept peacefully."

"This is so good." Both paused for seconds then William asked "Do you have any plan for tonight?"

Ishtar, who was happy, said "No, no I am free."

"Can I pick you up tonight." before Ishtar said a word William asked "What time can I see you?"

"Mmmmm, I do not know."

"Okay I will see you before 9 o'clock." Ishtar said nothing while William said "bye now and take care."

"Bye." Ishtar said kindly. She was happy and very excited. She smiled and stayed silent and alone in her room for a minute. Before she put her cell phone away she started asking herself how William got her phone's number. People, who have her cell phone's number, are her sister and some of her co_ workers and those people do not know William.

There is only one person, who knows William and can give him the number, the person is Maria. Immediately she called her "Did you give my cell phone's number to William?" Ishtar was curious

"Who is William?" Maria asked

Ishtar smiled "You know who he is."

"Who is he?"

"He is the man, who dropped me home last night."

"Did you talk to him?" Maria asked passionately

"Yes, I did."

"What was the conversation about?"

"He asked about my health."

"What else?"

"He asked me to go out with him."

"You said yes, right?"

"Yes, I said yes and I am going tonight with him."

"I am so happy."

Ishtar smiled then she said "I have to go now. I am so hungry."

"Okay but you have to tell me all the details later."

"Yes, I will." Ishtar said then she ended the call. She stayed sitting on her bed for minutes and thinking what to wear tonight. Suddenly her her sister got into the room

"Are you okay?" Ishtar's sister asked

"Yes." Ishtar replied

"Are you going to eat your breakfast?"

Ishtar stood up "Yes, I will." Then she announced "i am going outside tonight."

"Going where?"

"With someone."

"Are you going on a date?"

"Yes."

"How?"

"What do you mean by how?"

"You do not like dating and we want to stay forever virgin."

"I am waiting for right person who I will marry."

"Maybe the right person never exists."

"Yes, he does." Ishtar said while her sister said nothing then Ishtar got out of the room. Her sister, who was following her, asked her "What is his name?"

"William."

"Where did you meet him?"

"Where is mother?" Ishtar asked when she entered the kitchen and did not see her mother

"She is in the balcony." Ishtar's sister said then she asked when they sat on a table "Is he your co-worker?"

"No."

"Is he your chef?"

Ishtar looked at her and said madly "No."

"Is he handsome?"

"Yes." Ishtar said then she looked at her and said "Please stop asking questions. I want to eat."

"I want to know everything."

"I will tell you later, I have to eat now then prepare for tonight." Ishtar's sister said nothing while Ishtar started eating.

After more than an hour Ishtar took a shower and started preparing herself to meet William, but she was confused about the clothes although she called her sister for a help

"You have never been confused about clothes."

"I know." Ishtar said while she was standing infront of closet looking at the clothes

Ishtar's sister stepped forward and stood beside her "Wear this blue jeans," her sister suggested while she was pointing at blue jeans which was folded on the closet shelf

"It is too casuel."

"It is first date. You have to be comfortable."

Ishtar looked at her "I can not believe I am taking advice from my younger sister."

Her sister sat on a bed and said angry "Okay you can were what ever you want."

Ishtar sighed then she said "whatever I will wear it." Ishtar wore with her jeans, a black sweater and a black jacket.

William was waiting outside standing against his car. He smiled when he saw Ishtar coming "You look gorgeous." William said happily then he opened his car's front door for Ishtar to sit while Ishtar sat in the front seat and said kindly "Thanks."

William asked when he got into the car "Do you want to go to a specific place?"

Ishtar said "No."

"Okay." William smiled and started driving

It was Christmas time, everywhere was decorated, trees, windows, and houses. Everything was colourful. The stores were also busy. Some people were buying gifts; others were walking on side walk. People were full of energy, life and joyful.

Ishtar was one of them. She was so excited and happy. She looked at the street and asked William "Can we walk here?" Ishtar referred her index finger of the right hand toward people.

William looked at the people and "Yea, sure. But can we drink coffee first, and then we will walk here."

"Yea." Ishtar smiled

William parked his car and then they walked beside each other. When they reached a coffee shop Ishtar entered first then William followed her. Ishtar sat on a table while William was waiting for their order. She looked happily at people and the light of decoration. She lowered her head and smiled. She remembered what happened to her last night during her shift at the bar

"Why are you smiling?" William asked when he was caming back to her and holding two cups of coffee.

Ishtar raised her head "I remembered what happened last night when we were in the bar."

William set the cups of coffee on the table and said while he was sitting "At beginning I thought you fainted."

"If l fell down in front of people, I would be so embarrass. You just saved me."

William said with a smile "You have to relax and take care of yourself." Then he passed her cup of coffee to her

"I will never ever climb that place again, even though you will be setting there."

"Do not worry. I will be ready to hold you again." William smiled and took a sip from his coffee while Ishtar's face blushed shyly, and she avoided William's eyes and started playing in her hair to reduce her nervousness

"How is your coffee?" William changed the subject of the conversation thus Ishtar can feel comfortable

"Perfect." She said then she asked "Can I ask you question?"

"Sure."

"Who gave you my cell phone's number?"

William smiled "I told you Santa." Ishtar smiled then she brushed her face away from his eyes "your friend, who works with you, gave it to me." William confessed

"I knew that." Ishtar cheered

"Did you ask her?" William asked

"Yes, but she did not give me the answer."

William drank from his coffee then he looked at Ishtar, whom was looking outside and asked her "If you want, we can leave."

"Yes, I am ready." Ishtar said then her cell phone rang. It was her sister. She sighed and did not answer while the phone kept ringing.

"You can answer it." William said

"It is my sister."

"You can talk to her; I will be waiting here for you."

Ishtar smiled then she stood up and got out of coffee shop to answer her phone

"Hurry! come home and help me." Her sister said sadly

"What happened?" Ishtar asked and her voice full of fear

"It is disaster….. My mom is not feeling well. She can not breathe." Her sister was crying

"Okay, I am in my way." Ishtar said sadly then she breathed out deeply then she said herself "I have very bad luck i know that." She got into the coffee shop sadly and walked toward William

"What happened?" William asked Ishtar when he saw her sad face then he stood beside her

Ishatr looked at him and said "I am so sorry but i have to go…. My mom … something happened to her."

"Does she need a doctor?" William was concerned

"I do not know." Ishtar was sad then they got out of the store and walked silent to William's car

"What did exactly your sister said?" William asked when he started driving

"Something bad happened to my mother." Ishtar said then she stayed silent while William looked sadly at her.

"Do not worry, only few minutes left and then we will reach home." William tried to comfort her "As soon as we reach the bulding i will call an ambulance."

"I hope we do not need the ambulance."

He asked after seconds of silent "Is she ill?"

Ishtar sighed "Yes."

William hurried and opened the door for her as soon as they reached Ishtar's building while Ishtar said to him "Thank you."

"I am coming with you. Maybe you need help."

"No thanks." Ishtar said when she stood opposite him beside his car "I am so sorry for ruining our first date."

William looked at her and said kindly and sweetly "Do not think about tonight we have countless days ahead of us to go again on a date. If you need any help, just call me."

Ishtar looked lovely at him then she walked quickly, while William watched her until she disappeared. As soon as Ishtar entered the apartment she looked at her mother, who seemed as corpse laying down on the floor while her sister was sitting beside her crying

"Did you call an ambulance?"

"Yes, I did."

Ishtar sat beside her sister waiting for the ambalance. Just few minutes passed the ambulance came in. They got their mother while Ishtar and her sister followed them with Maria, who was driving her car behind the ambulance

After two hours Maria and Ishtar were waiting in waiting room in a hospital

"So your first date ended up in hospital." Maria said

Ishtar looked sad at her "Yea, I am very frustrated."

"Do not worry, you can uncount today and erased from your calendar."

"It is unforgettable." Ishtar said then they stayed silent for minutes after that William called Ishtar and asked about her mother

"She is fine now. We are in a hospital with her." Ishtar's voice was normal "She was poisoned. She ate soup which was leftover from days." She explained then she said kindly "Thanks for your call."

William said "I am so happy to hear that." Then he added after he heard her yawning "I believe you have to rest. I will call you tomorrow." Then they ended the call.

After few minutes Ishtar's sister joined them in a waiting room and said while she was sitting "She is sleeping now."

Ishtar looked at her "That was scary."

"Yes it was." they looked at each other and both sighed then Ishtar's sister said "the doctor said tomorrow she can leave the hospital."

"This is good." Ishtar said happily

"Okay I have to leave now." Maria stood up then she said "Tomorrow before you come to the hospital you have to tell so we can get your mother out of here."

"Yes, I will." Ishtar stood beside her

"Okay, bye now."

"Thanks." Ishtar said kindly while Maria smiled then she walked alone far from them then Ishtar sat beside her sister

"How was your date?" Ishtar's sister asked

"You called when my date started." Ishtar said sadly then she added "This is not good sign."

"Again you start counting the sign."

"I always believe in signs."

Ishtar is superstitious. She used to count signs years ago and now she started again counting with William. First time William asked her out she rejected him and when she went with him on a date her mother got poisoned. She hoped next time if they go on a date, it will go well.

Chapter Three

FIRST KISS

On Friday, Ishtar left the library as soon as she could. She went home and relaxed for few hours then she called a taxi to drop her at a bar because Maria left the city for Christmas' vacation. Now she is all by herself.

On the same night William was busy. He shaved his beard and cut his hair. He knew Ishtar is alone tonight because Maria told him about her trip. He waited her to call him, but she did not call so he headed to the bar to see her. When they saw each other they waved in their hands with a smile. William left the bar for short time twice during Ishtar's shift, and then he came back and stayed there until Ishtar finished her shift. When Ishtar got out of changing room, she saw William waiting for her. She smiled then they walked side by side to his car. The sky was dark and it was raining, before they got out of the bar, Ishtar opened her back bag and got out it her umbrella. Then they walked together to William's car. William was holding the umbrella in his left hand while his right hand was on Ishtar's shoulder. Both breathed a sigh of relief when they got into the car. They looked at each other and smiled after second of silent Ishtra said while William was turning on the car "Did Maria tell you I am alone?"

"Yes. She did." he replied then he looked at her and asked her when he saw her yawning "Are you tired?"

"No, I am fine." She repiled Then she asked quickly "What did Maria tell you?" she was curious

William replied when he strated driving "She just answered my questions about you."

"About me!" She wanted passiontly to know everything.

"Yes." William focused on driving while Ishtar looked at him waiting to tell her every single word that he talked about her with Maria but William said nothing.

Ishtar looked upset, and then she yawned and rested her head on the window and closed her eyes while William looked at her and smiled after few seconds Ishtar looked at the sky and said "I guess it stopped raining."

William looked at the sky "I think it did." Then William changed the car direction while Ishtar asked after she noticed it is not the same street that leads her to her apartment "Where are we going?"

"I do not know." William smiled then he added "I do not want to go home, if you want, we can walk here." William parked his car then looked at Ishtar waiting for answer

"I hope it is not cold." Ishtar said

William looked at the sky then he got his hand out from the window. "It is drizzling rain but there is no wind."

"Let me check." Ishtar moved close to William's side and got her left hand out of the window. William looked at her and smiled her hair while Ishtar said withdrew slowly herself then she said "Okay, let go."

"I am going to take a parking ticket." William said then he got out of the car then got the umbrella from the back seat. When he came back, he opened Ishtar's door and threw the ticket inside.

As soon as Ishtar got out of the car, she inhaled the air while William locked the car and held the umbrella in his left hand while his right hand surrounded her arms. They started walking silently then William moved the umbrella away from her head which made a few drops of rain fell off on her hair "What are you doing?"

William smiled "by mistake."

Ishtar looked at him then she released her arms from William's hand and started walking alone "I believe I do not need the umbrella any more."

"You will be sick." William said

Ishtar started walking in front of William then she turned her face to him and opened her arms and looked at sky then she ran back to William to get under the umbrella again "oh, one drop fell in my eye." She said while she was rubbing her right eye by her right hand.

William smiled "Are you okay."

"Yes I am."

Then they walked silently. There were few people there. Some of them were inside the bus shelter, others were walking.

"Can we consider today a date?" William asked while he was looking at Ishtar. They stopped then gazed at each other "Yes it is." She replied warmly

"Let's go somewhere better than staying here," William suggested

"I am starving." Ishtar announced then they started walking back to the car

"Look at this." Ishtar pointed at a small spot in the corner of the street which was full of water. She moved quickly toward it and kicked the water by her right foot, which made the water splashed on William, who was behind her.

"What are you doing?" William said while he was pointing at his clothes

Ishtar turned her face at him. She smiled "I am full of energy."

"Yea, you are." William said while he was nodding his head and smiling

"If my mother knows where I am at this time and with a man, she will be very upset."

"You live with her, right?"

"Yea, my sister and I live with my mother and she has very strict rules for us."

"My mother keeps reminded me I am getting old and have no girlfriend."

"My mother does not know i work in a bar."

"I have to spend every Sunday with her so she can ask me about my dating life."

"My mother hates staying Sundays at home and do not allow us to relax."

"She makes me to go shopping with her which it is the most things i hate."

Ishtar though for seconds then she said "oh yea, I remembered I saw you once getting out of woman's clothes with a woman."

"And I was holding bags full of clothes in my both hands. The woman was my mother." William said with a sigh

"She wants me to go every Sunday to church although I do not practice."

"She makes me watch the boring show on Sundays that she watches so she can remind me I have to have family." Both laughed on their mothers then they got into the car and headed to restaurant so they can end their starvation.

This was the first time that William shared his thoughts and complaint about his mother to a woman. Ishtar's complainning encouraged him to talk about his mother and tell her she in not the only one that she suffers from her mother. In the end, both seemed their mothers have very difficult rules.

After they finished eating William drove Ishtar home. The sun was already rose and Ishtar had to relax and rest so she work again tonight. Her mother and sister were still asleep. She breathed a sigh of relief and said herself "no lecture today."

She took a shower then went to her room. She opened the door smiling then walked slowly to her bed while looking at her sister. She got into the bed slowly and slept peacefully.

When Ishtar woke up it was already noontime. She unveiled her face and looked at her sister's bed. She yawned then rose her head "Good morning."

Her sister looked at her "Good morning."

Ishtar threw the blanket away and sat on her bed "I am so tired."

"How was your night yesterday?"

Ishtar smiled and said happily "Great."

"Really! You were all by yourself." Her sister, who was nail polishing her fingers, was surprise

Ishtar yawned again then replied "Yes, it was."

Her sister looked puzzeled at her while Ishtar explained "someone dropped me home."

"Who?"

Ishtar smiled then she said "Do you remember when mom got poisoned?"

Her sister nodded her head and said unhappy "Yes, of course."

"He dropped me home last night. But before I came home I went with him on a date."

Ishtar's sister eyes opened widely then she asked "Do you mean yesterday was the second date?"

"Yes."

"Oh, I thought you said he may not call you again."

"Yea, this is what i thought but i was wrong."

Her sister got off the bed and walked toward her "I want to know the details."

Ishtar adjusted herself and moved close to her sister "he was waiting me at the bar then I went with him after I finished working."

"And…." Ishtar's sister was curious

"Before he dropped me home, he told me this is consided a date so before I came home, we walked then we ate breakfast." Ishtar was happy

"What did you eat?"

Ishtar shook her head in disbelief "Nothing!"

Her sister looked disappointed "When will you see him again?"

"Today."

At that time their mother entered the room while Ishtar's phone rang

"Who are you going to see today?" their mother asked them

They looked at each other while Ishtar's phone kept ringing "Nobody." Ishtar said

"I heard you are going to see someone."

"Oh, it is my manager. I want a day off for christmas." Ishtar said after seconds of thought

Thier mother looked at them then she asked Ishtar "Why are you not answering your phone?"

"I will do later. They are from work." At that moment Ishtar phone received a message

"I want to go outside so one of you will come with me."

"I can not. I am so hungry and I have to prepare for my work." Ishtar said while she was reading the message on her phone

Ishtar's sister looked unhappy at her then she said to her mom "Okay, we will go together. You can go and change." then she looked at Ishtar and whispered "later I need an update."

Ishtar said nothing she just ran to the washroom so she can get herself ready to meet William. She ate then wore warm clothes. She left the apartment and got out of the building. William was waiting her in time. He smiled then he opened the door for her.

"How many hours do you have left until you start your shift?" William asked Ishtar when they sat in the car while Ishtar looked at her watch and started calculating "I have over five hours left"

"Okay, this is perfect." William looked at her and asked "Do you like movies?"

"Yes, I do." Ishtar said happily

"Which kind of movies you like?"

Ishtar hesitated then she said "comedies and romance movies." Then she added quickly "also fantasy and some actions."

William smiled "Okay, let's go and see a movie."

There were a lot of people lined up for tickets. The place was crowded.

"You choose the movie." William said to Ishtar, while Ishtar looked rapidly at the screen and picked (What Women Want) which was starred by Mel Gibson and Helen Hunt and it was recently released

"Okay, I got What Women Want' tickets." William said when he returned to Ishtar, who was waiting him.

"When will the movie start?" she asked him

"After fifteen minutes from now." William said then they walked together to see the movie after they bought popcorn. They sat in the last line. Ishtar was laughing most of the time on the movie while William was watching her.

"Did you like the movie?" William asked Ishtar when they got out of theatre

"I loved it." Ishtar said happily

"Do you think women need a man, who knows everything about them? A man who can read their mind."

"It is not necessary to know everything about your partner to make a good relationship." Ishtar said then she added while William was looking at her "If you are responsible and respectful for your partner, the relationship will go on."

"If women and men tell each other what they need, I believe at this time we do not need to read others mind to understand them." William said after he got into the car

Ishtar agreed with him "Yea, I believe being honest and respectful is the key for everything and sometimes we need someone to read our mind."

William started driving then he looked at Ishtar and asked "so you need someone to read your mind."

Ishtar thought for seconds then she said "Yea, I think I do."

"Why?"

"So I do not have to argue or repeat something over and over."

"If he can read your mind, he will be what you want him to be." William said

"No, he still has to do what he wants."

"But you still want him to do what you want when he read your mind."

"Yes."

"Why?"

"By doing what other want, we guarantee not losing them."

William looked at her and asked her "Are you afraid of losing someone?"

"I think we all afraid of losing something or someone." William looked at her and said nothing.

After minutes they stopped and got into a restaurant to eat

"How is your job in the library?" William asked after they ordered food

"It is good."

"Do you like working there?"

"Yes, I do," Ishtar opened her purse and wrote the address for William "Maybe, one day you want to borrow a book." Ishtar gave the paper for William, who said while he was taking the paper "I will borrow a book that you will pick for me."

"Okay, as long as I work in children section, the book will be from there."

"You work in children section," William was surprise

Ishtar smiled "yes, I do." Then she added "It is good job, but you have to be patient with them especially on Wednesdays I read a story for them."

"A story!" William was surprised

"Yes, then I answer their question."

"I guess you adore kids."

"I believe being parent it is the hardest job." William nodded his head for agreement

At that time the waiter came with a food

"Do you have sibling?" Ishtar asked

"Yes, I do one brother, who is the youngest and still living with my mother and sister, who lives alone in her apartment."

"And your father."

"I have never met my father. He left my mother when she was pregnant." William was normal and calm while Ishtar seemed unhappy "I am sorry." She said while William just continued eating. She wanted to ask him more questions about his childhood but she felt he was not interested as a result she kept silent. After few minutes they got out the restaurant and headed to Ishtar's work place.

"I have to leave now. I have things to do. When you finish, I will be here." William said to Ishtar when they were standing infront of the bar

"Okay, thanks." Ishtar said then she got into the bar while William got into his car and left the place.

The time was passing so slowly. Ishtar was very bored and felt lonely. Every half an hour she was looking at her watch or at the doors in order to not miss seeing William when he will come. Finally William came on when she finished her shift. Ishtar was leaving when he opened the bar's door.

"Am I late?" William seemed unhappy

"I thought you are not coming." Ishtar looked worried

"I never do that." William said kindly "I am sorry for coming late."

"It is fine." Ishtar smiled

William smiled "I was so busy. I am sorry again."

"I hope you enjoyed in your time, did you not?" Ishtar said as soon as they got into the car.

"I met my friend. What about you?"

"I was so bored." Then she looked at him and asked "Do you spend the whole time with your friend?"

William replied after seconds of thinking "No, I called my mother and went to my apartment. In the end I came back to the bar."

"You saw your mother!"

"Yea, only for a half an hour." William said then he looked at Ishtar smiling and said "I guess you were bored because you were not with me."

"Yes and no." Ishtar hesitated before she replied while William looked at her confused wile Ishtar said "I enjoy being with you and I miss Maria."

"So you enjoy being with Maria more than being with me."

"No." Ishtar said immediately then she added "But she is the only person that I know."

"She is your best friend, right?"

"She is the only friend that I have."

"And take care of you."

"I believe she told you the story of my life."

William shook his head for agreement "we did talk about you."

"I hope she told you the good thing."

William smiled "she did." Then he asked "Do you have any plan for tomorrow?"

"No. I have to stay home with my mother."

"Is she sick?"

"No, she is not, but my sister is going to be out of house and my mother has some plans so I have to be with her."

"Is she old?"

"Not that old but she is sick."

"Is she a divorced woman, or a widow?"

"Divorce is very seldom in my community, and the idea is not accepted in the society."

"Wait, wait," William was surprised and confused "Why is the divorce banned in your community?"

"It is not just banned in my community; most women in my community do not get divorce because no one supports them."

William looked at her in disbelief "If you change your mind about tomorrow just calls me." Ishtar shook her head for agreement while William added "I guess I will spend my day tomorrow with my mother or a freind."

Ishtar looked at him "I hope you will enjoy being with your mother."

"Oh yea I will. When she will see me alone tomorrow, he will say another Christmas pass and no woman."

Ishtar smiled while William added "I guess I should read a book which it is not good idea."

"Why?"

"I only read a book when I am in airplane."

"Mostly, I read in winter."

"Why do you read in winter?"

"Because it is boring and long season."

"Not really. You still can enjoy it."

"How?"

"You can do ice staking."

"I can not do skiing."

"This is bad I want to do skiing with you."

Ishtar looked at him and said "We can do something else."

"Yea, I guess."

"Why does your mother keep reminding you of having a family?" Ishtar asked after few seconds of silence

"I guess I am old." William said then he looked at Ishtar "I think I am so old for you."

"No, no, you are not." She regretted her question and kept silent then she looked at William, who was silent, she closed her eyes and yawned "I am so tired, the bar was so busy."

"We almost arrived." William announced

William got off the car and opened the door for Ishtar and walked with her on her way to her apartment. This was the first time that he walked with her and Ishtar wondered about his walking with her. Before she opened the door of the building, she looked at William and said "Good night."

William smile and said "good night." Then he walked silently to his car while Ishtar looked at him until he disappeared. She felt he was sad and disappointed. Two things she did made him sad. The converstion about his age and refusing his invatation to spend Christams with him, she hopes everything will go well after that night.

On Sunday, it was Christmas Eve. It was snowing outside. A few people were outside William woke up late and went to his mother's house at noon. As always during lunch time all of them gathered around the table to eat. William's mother was sitting beside her husband while Jessica and her brother were sitting opposite them. William beside an empty chair which her mother used to set beside him to remind him he is still single

"Next year, you will turn forty." Margaret, William's mother, said to him when the family were eating.

William sighed "I know."

"And you do not even have a girlfriend! "

"I have." William announced

"You have…." Margaret and Jessica said at the same time.

"Yes, I have." William confirmed

"Why did you not bring her with you today?" her mother, who disbelieved him, asked

"We just started dating."

"Soon you will break up with her." Margaret said

"I do not think that will happen." William said

"If you like her, you should bring her with you."

William said after seconds of thought "You will meet her one day."

"Do we know her?" Margret asked

"I do not think you know her."

"Is she beautiful?" Jessica asked

"Yes, she is." William said smoothly and the smile was on his face.

"I hope she is the last one," Margaret said while William did not respond then she asked after second of silent "Are you serious in your relationship?"

"I just started seeing her."

"You will get married, will not you?"

"I did not mention married."

"I will be your best man." His youngest brother, who was sitting beside him on left side, said

"I will be one of your bridesmaids." William's sister said

William looked at them and shook his head in disbelief "I knew I will have those questions again."

Margaret looked at William and said sweetly "I can not wait to see her."

William looked at her "Maybe you will see her."

"So you are serious." Margaret said

"I said we just started dating," William, who was upset, said then he added sadly while he was standing "Can you stop taking about me, please"

"Did you finish eating?" his mother asked

"Yes, I did."

His mother looked at his plate which there was still food in it "You did not eat your food."

"I was not hungry." William kissed his mother's head

"Are you okay?" His mother asked

"I am just tired and i have to make a call." William said then walked far from his mother. After few seconds his mother followed him "I am sorry for making you upset. Today is Christmas and I want you to be happy."

William smiled "You are my mother and I will never be upset from you."

"There is plenty of food if you want to eat."

"Okay, I just have to make a call then I will decide." William said while his mother smiled and returned back to food table

"Is he upset?" Jessica asked her mother

"No he is not." Her mother said while she was sitting

"I thought he is going to date Julia?" Jessica seemed sad

"She is only a friend for him."

"She stayed in his apartment several times."

"I believe things did not go well between them."

"She will be devastated."

"She has to see someone else."

"She loves him and cares about him."

"And he cares about someone else."

After few minutes William joined them

"Are you staying with us tonight, or you have another plan?" William's mother asked

"I gusee I am staying." William sat on a chair "I sent messages and made a call but there is no respond." William seemed upset

"Who did you call?" Margaret asked

"My girlfriend."

"Is she coming?"

"She did not respond yet? I guess she is busy." William seemed upset

"You can see her later."

"Tomorrow afternoon I am going out of city."

"I guess you can celebrate New Years Eve with her."

"Yea, I will."

"Does she have party tonight?"

"No, she is with her sick mother."

"Oh, do not worry tonight you are going to enjoy." William's mother said

"What is going on tonight?"

"I invite few people. It is not going to be crowded i know you do not like being among many people." William mother said

"I think I want stay until the end."

"You can stay as long as you want." Margaret said while William smiled

On New Years Eve Ishtar was standing beside the window of her room looking outside. She was bored and upset. She did not see or contact William for days because he was out of city for business. She sighed and kept looking outside hoping for something to happen

"You forgot your phone in the kitchen." Ishtar's sister said when she entered their room. Ishtar looked at her sister "Your phone received two messages." Her sister added "......and I already read them." She hesitated before she confessed

Ishtar moved toward her sister "Why did you read the messages?" Ishtar was angry

"Give me my phone." Ishtar stretched her right hand

"William is the sender?" Ishtar's sister said

Ishtar sat on dege of her bed while the phone was in her hand

"Are you going to see him tonight?" Ishtar's sister asked

Ishtar replied while she was reading the messages "maybe!"

"Is he romantic?"

Ishtra looked at her sister "I think he is. We started dating recently."

"My boyfriend is romantic."

"Is he?"

"Yes, he is." Her sister said then she added after seconds of thought "By the way I slept with him."

"What?" Ishtar was shocked

"Yes, I did." Ishtar's sister seemed worry

"It is your body and your choice. It belongs to you and it is not my body or my property."

"Oh really! I thought you will be angry." Ishtar's sister was surprise

"No, I am not. Everything is yours."

"Actully I slept will him long time ago but I was afraid to tell you."

"I am not." Ishtar said loudly then she whispered "Just do not let my mother knows."

Ishtar's sister smiled "I know." Ishtar also smiled then her sister said while Ishtar was still busy on her cell phone "Can I meet him?"

Ishtar looked at her "Who?

"Your boyfriend."

"Why?" Ishtar was surprise

"I just want to see him."

"One day, you will see him." Ishtar said while she was standing

"Are you going to see him tonight?" Ishtar's sister asked

"Yes, I am." Ishtar said then she added happily "I want to celebrate New Years Eve with him."

"Okay I will stay with our mother."

"Thank you. I have to find perfect clothes." Ishtar said while she was walking toward the closet

"When are you going to see him?"

"After an hour."

"You still have time to choose."

Ishtar opened the closet "I know."

This is going to be the first time that Ishtar will spend New Years Eve with someone other than her mother, sister and Maria. They usually stay home and celebrate alone.

"Where do you want to go?" William asked Ishtar when they got into the car

"I do not know." Ishtar seemed excited

"This is your first new year eve celebrating outside your home, right?

"Yea."

"It will be unforgatable." William said with a smile then he continued driving

"Where are we going?"

"It is surprise. You will enjoy it." William said while Ishtar smiled

William drove over an hour then he parked his car. He talked to a man, gave him his car key then left the parking area. It was very crowded and windy. William held Ishtar's hand and started walking carefully. It was the happiest time for Ishtar. Every time when they crossed the street, Ishtar got very close to William. Finally they reached Time Square

"Why did not you tell me we will be here?" Ishtar released William's hand and started looking at the building

"I said it is surprise." William smiled then he added "I hope you like it."

Ishtar looked at him and said with a big smile "Are you joking? Being here it was a dream. It is amazing."

"I am glad to hear that. Any time you want we can come here."

Ishtar looked at him "With my busy life I can not go further than the library."

They walked for five minutes then they stopped and entered a bar

"Are you cold?" William said when he saw Ishtar was rubbing her shoulder when they were sittig on a table

"I was, now I am feeling better."

"You can relax we will stay here. The bar helps us to see and access to Ball Drop." William said then he asked Ishtar while he was looking at the menu "What do you want for drink?"

"I do not drink." Ishtar announced

"What?" William looked at her. He was surprised while Ishtra smiled

"Well I drink only one glass of beer or wine in every three months."

William was shocked "Really!"

"Yes."

"But, you work in a bar."

"Yea, but I do not drink."

"Tonight you have to drink." William said with a smile then the waiterss came and talked to William while Ishtar noticed William ordered for her a beer same as he ordered for him

"What did you say to your mother when you left house?" William asked

"I told her I have to work."

William smiled "She believed you."

"I think she did." Ishtar said then she added "I can not tell her the truth. She will start yelling then she panic and this is not good for her health." Ishtar explained then she asked after seconds of silent "Do you travel alot?"

"No few times a year." William ordered another drink then he looked at Ishtar's drink "It is new years eve. You have to drink."

"I am."

"I told my mother about you." William announced

Ishtar looked surprise "what did you told her?"

"I said I am dating."

"What did she say?" Ishtar was anxious

"She said she want to meet you." Ishtar looked at him in disbelief and said nothing while William announced "we have to leave now the count down will start soon."

They did not walk far from the bar. The place was crowded and William was holding Ishtar's right hand tight. Ishtar looked at people around her. There were families and couples then she looked at William and smiled. The crowd started counting Ishtar looked at William, who was counting happily she smiled and started counting. Confetti dropped as throngs of revelers cheer the start of 2001 in New York City's Times Square. William held Ishtar's face in his both hands and kissed her. Ishtar riveted in her place.

This was the first time that William kissed her. She said nothing and smiled to him. She was happy. Then he kissed her again at this time Ishtar kissed him back. It was amazaing and unforgettable moment. William released her face and looked at her "Happy New Year." He said happily

"Happy New Year." Ishtar said then she started laughing when confetti kept dropping on them

William smiled "You are so beautiful when you laugh."

Ishtar looked at him and smiled. She held his hands and said "Thanks for making my New Year's Eve special and unique."

William looked at her and kissed her again then he held her right hand and walked back to the bar which it was crowed and noise as a result William and Ishtar had to speak loudly tp hear each other

"I need more drink." He said

"I think I want a drink as well." Ishtar said while William looked at her and smiled.

Ishtar had a glass of wine while William had tequila shots

"Do you want a shot?" William said after he drank his shot

"No, I do not."

"What was your plan for tonight before I contacted you?"

Ishtar yawned "Nothing just staying home."

"You are tired, are not you?" William was concerned

"No, I am okay." Ishtar said and yawned again "What did you say to your mother about me?" Ishtar asked

"I told her I have a girlfriend then she said she wants to meet you."

"What did you say?"

"Nothing." William said then he smiled and held her right hand "We are leaving."

"Can we stay longer?"

"Are you not tired?"

"No, I am good."

"Okay we can stay longer." William said then he ordered more drink

After an hour they left. They were walking hardly among the crowd William kept holding Ishtar's hand until they reach a hotel. William looked at her and announced "We are going to sleep here."

"What?" Ishtar was surprised

"We will leave tomorrow. We need to rest." William said when they got into the hotel

"When did you arrange all of these?" Ishtar asked him when they got into the elevator

"After Christmas." William confessed with a smile then they stopped and got out of elevator. They walked few steps then William stopped and said "This is your room and this is my room." William said while he was pointing on two doors' rooms next to each other "If you need any thing just knock my door room."

Ishtar looked at him and smiled "Thanks for everything."

William kissed her forhead then he said "Good night."

"Good night." Each one of them got into a different room

William's decision by getting separated room for Ishtar was unimaginable. Everything he did tonight was humble and a true gentleman. It will always be in Ishtar's memories

Chapter Four

MEETING THE FAMILY

Days passed William and Ishtar s continued seeing each other and Maria came back from her vacation.On Wednesday, February, fourteenth was Valentine's Day. William sent to Ishtar's apartment flowers and promised her the real valentine will be on Sunday.

"Are you going to see him?" Ishtar's sister asked when she saw Ishtar standing infront of the closet

"Yes" Ishtar replied

"Can I see him, please?" Ishtar's sister begged

"No." Ishtar said sharply

"It will be only for a minute, please." Ishtar's sister begged again

Ishtar sighed "Okay, you can see him." then she looked at the closet and said "I am confused about the clothes."

"Again clothes." Ishtar's sister said while Ishtar looked unhappy at her "A dress is good." Ishtar's sister suggested

"Yes a dress." Ishtar cheered

She wore a black long dress which it has long sleeves and with it she wore black pantyhose. Her jacket was long brown which it matched with her brown flat short boot.

"Happy delayed Valentine's day." William, who was waiting outside the building, said with asmile

Ishtar looked happily at him and smiled "Happy delayed valentine day."

William said while he was looking at her "You are stunning."

"Thank you…… can you wait for few minutes. My sister wants to see you."

"Sure." William was surprised while Ishtar waved to a girl, whom was waiting inside the building and looking at them, to come in. When she came in, Ishtar introduced her sister to William.

"Later when you return to home, you have to tell me what your sister says about me." William said when they got into the car

"You really want to know?" Ishtar was surprised

"Yea, I want to know."

"Sure, I will tell you her opinion about you."

"My mother asked me about you." William said

"What did you tell her?" Ishtar was surprised

"I told her I am going to spend my delayed valentine's day with her." William looked at Ishtar and smiled

"Why did she ask you about me?"

"She want to know if I am still dating or not."

"What did she say?"

"Nothing, she was happy." William said while Ishtar smiled and said nothing

After few minutes Ishtar looked at the road and asked "Where are we going?"

"I do not know. I am just driving."

"What?" Ishtar said

"I am just joking." William smiled "We are going to eat."

It was a big restaurant, lighted by candles. There was a fountain in the middle. The fountain is a dancing woman and the water is coming from her standard. Beside the fountain there was a man singing and behind the singer were three others men, who were playing a classical music.

William asked after he ordered the food and drink for them "Do you like the place?"

"Yes I do." Ishtar said happily

"By the way my apartment is near this restaurant."

"Oh yea." Ishtar said

"I will give you the address, and you can visit me any time you want." William said then he asked a waiter, who brought food for them a pen and paper. William wrote the address and gave it to Ishtar

"Okay, sure." Ishtar replied while she was putting the address in her purse

After few minutes William looked at Ishtar's glass of wine and said "You drink over half of your glass."

Ishtar smiled "I drink every week now."

"I will get you another one." William said while Ishtar nodded her head for agreement.

There were a few couple dancing on that calm and slow music. William looked at them and then said while he was standing and stretching his right hand to Ishtar "Let's dance."

"I am not a good dancer." Ishtar said shyly while she was looking around her

"Who told you I am an excellent dancer?" William grabbed her hand then they walked to dancing floor.

William surrounded Ishtar's waist in his arms, while Ishtar's hands surrounded William's neck and her head on his chest.

"You are so tall." Ishtar said

William smiled then he looked at her face "and you are so short."

"I am not short, you are tall." Ishtar looked serious

"Yes, you are not short. I am so tall." William said with smile

"I am wearing flat shoes." Ishtar tried

"You may be short girl but you just take my breath away." William whispered warmly in her left ear while Ishtar opened her mouth to say something but she said nothing. They just danced silently. After few minutes they went back to their table.

"William, I can not believe I am seeing you after all of this time." A man, who was standing with a woman in front of them, said

William raised his head then smiled while Ishtar looked curious at both of them

"Patrick! What a surprise." William said happily while he was standing then he looked at Ishtar and said "This is my girlfriend, Ishtar." Then William pointed at Patrick and said to Ishtar "This is my best freind Patrick and his wife Lisa."

Ishtar smiled and shook their hands while William said "You can join us."

Patrick and his wife pulled chairs and sat with them

"How is everything?" Patrick asked

"Busy." William said

"How long have been dating?" Patrick asked happily

"Since last year." William replied

"How did you meet?" Lisa, who seemed excited, asked

"We met in a bar." William said then he looked at Patrick and said "I am calling you on your phone number and office number but there is no answer."

Patrick sighed "It is long story. I am working in different place now. I am now working at Centre's Bank locates in North World Trade Centres and the bank locates on 101st floor." Patrick took a deep breath then he said "My daughter threw my cell phone in washroom and I lost all the numbers." Patrick said

"Okay, I understood." William said then he called a waitres and ordered food and drink

"Why did not you visit me at home?" Patrick asked

"I did not think about it."

"You should visit us together." Lisa suggested while she was looking at Ishtar

William looked at Ishtar, whom seemed surprise then he said "Yea, I think we will come together."

"We should plan to go out on a double date." Lisa said while she was looking at Ishtar

"Okay, we can go." Ishtar, who was so confused and lost, said

At that time waiters came in with drinks and food as soon as the waiters left William asked "How many kids do you have now?"

"Oh, recently I have a son."

"Congratulation," William said happily then he asked "how old is he?"

"A month."

"His baptism is in April. You can join us both of you." Lisa said

William smiled and nodded his head for agreement then Patrick got from his pocket his wallet and got two pictures from it. He gave them to William while he was saying "A picture of a kid, who is riding a pony, is Olivia. She is four year old and the other picture is David, who is new born."

William smiled then he passed the pictures to Ishtar "I can not believe you have two kids."

"Time flies William, hurry up." Patrick said while William smiled then Patrick added while he was looking at Ishtar "I know your boyfriend since we were in high school and he was very popular during that time." Ishtar smiled while Patrick added "When i got married ten years ago, your boyfriend was my best man." He stopped then he smiled while he was saying "and he dated one of Lisa's bridesmaids."

Lisa, who was surprise, said quickly "What? Who?"

William looked at Patrick "It was long time ago, I can not remember."

Patrick said "The shortest one. I can not remember her name."

"Oh, Ann." Lisa said

"How long did you stay together?" Patrick asked

"I can not remember. It was long time ago but you as always keep telling old stories." William said then he looked at Ishtar, whom was silent

"Old stories are the best." Patrick said

"Some time they are embarrassed." William said and looked again at Ishtar. He knew she got annoyed from this conversation so he asked immediately "What happened with a management? We talked about it when I saw you last time?"

"I do not want it." Patrick said

"Why?" William was surprise

"It is not a good idea." Lisa said

"Too much work and I am so busy with new born now." Patrick said

"You do not have to take it immediately."

"Really!"

"Yea, Next time I will help you with the plan when I will see you again." William said kindly

Patrick looked at William "How?"

"How long have you been working there?"

"Around eleven years."

"I know people there they can help you."

"Okay, you can visit me any time at World Trade Centre so we can discuess the management at my office." Patrick said then he gave his numbers to William and said "we have to leave now. The kids are with their grandmother." Patrick said then he stood up with his wife. They looked at Ishtar and said with a smile "Nice to meet you. We hope we can see you soon."

Ishtar smiled "see you." Then she watched them until they disappeared

After minutes of silence William looked worry at Ishtar and asked "Are you okay?"

"Yes, I am."

"You were silent the whole time."

"You saw your best friend and his wife, whom did not see them for long time,...." before Ishtar added a word William said "You did not like them, did you?"

"Why would not I like them?" Ishtar was surprised

"I do not know." William stopped "They were talking about me and my past."

"You just said your past." Ishtar stopped then she said sharply "It is already over, isn't it."

"Yes, it is." William hesitated then he asked "if I go to their kid baptism will you come with me!"

"Yes, I will." Then she added "But you will be my plus one at my sister's wedding."

"Your sister is getting married." William was surprised

"Well, she is only engaged now." Ishtar stopped then she added "I think she will get married next year."

"Wow that is fast."

"Yea, it will be small wedding I guess." Ishtar stopped then she raised her eyebrows "You and I will help her to find a dress."

"Why? I hate shopping?" William announced "I already told you before."

"I know but Maria is pregnant and she can not...."

"Maria pregnant!" William was shock

"Yes she is and she has morning sickness thus she can not help us."

"Wow, I guess I miss alot."

"Yea, it will be very busy summer."

William looked at her and said "Can we leave I think i need fresh air."

Ishtar said when they were leaving "I am sorry I did not want to stress you."

"Wow alot of occasions are coming in."

"Yea, I guess."

"I will be invited to baby shower, will I?" William said after they got into the car

Ishtar smiled "no, you will not." William breathed a sigh of relief "Women are only invited to the baby shower. There will be no men."

"This is perfect for me."

"I think Patrick's thoughts about management are right."

"Why?"

"Well he said too much work to do and I guess they are financially okay."

"They are but it is very good opportunity."

"Yes, it is. If it is me I will accept the job. I need money and i am very ambitious woman." Ishtar said

William looked confused at her and asked "Do women work because they need money, or because they do not want to stay home?"

"Most women work because the need of money." Ishtar explained then she added "and to competite with men."

"Compete with me!" William was surprised

"Yes."

"Why?"

"So we can show them we can do things as they do it."

"Everyone can do what he or she wants without being a competitor."

"Sometime you have to."

Suddenly William entered a parking area and parked the car. He looked at Ishtar and asked "Do you want to meet my mother?"

"Yes, I want."

"What about now?"

"Now." Ishtar was surprised

"Yes." William said

Ishtar looked at him and the thoughts occupied her mind. Today William met her sister then she met his friend and his wife then she shared her plans with him about her sister's wedding. She added his mother to the list. She looked at William and smiled "Okay, let's go." She said

William smiled and started driving. William was so happy that Ishtar decided to meet his mother as a result he started telling her what she will expect when they will reach home "My mother is desired to see you. She set an extra chair around the eating table and the chair is always beside me and always empty."

Ishtar looked confused "You can change your spot."

"Although I change my spot, the chair, which is beside me, is still empty. They already planed at home, in ordered to remind me that I have to bring my girlfriend with me when I see them." William explained

"Why do they do that?"

"I guess I am an old man and I have to get on track quickly."

"This is wierd."

"My mother does not so I can not complain."

"How long has she been doing that?"

William thought for seconds then he said "I think five or years ago."

"And everyone joins her."

"Yes."

Ishtar seemed unhappy and stayed silent for seconds before she asked "Is every one will be at home?"

"Yes. And nobody knows that we are going to meet them."

"What?" Ishtar was surprised and scared at the same time then she suggested "You can tell your mother that we are coming now."

"I want to surprise them." William said while Ishtar looked disappointed

"I do not like this surprise."

"Before I met you, I was spending my Sundays with them." William stopped then he said "I think i did not see my mother for over a month."

"We can wait now and call your mother to tell her, please."

"Why do I have to do that?"

Ishtar sighed "I am so nervous."

"You do not have to panic. Everyone wants to meet you, especially my mother." William tried to comfort her.

"Can you stop here please, I am thirsty and I need some water?" Ishtar asked William when she saw small store in plaza

William looked at her "Sure."

As soon as William parked his car, Ishtar ran to the store while William waited her outside of the store. After few minutes, Ishtar came back. William held her face in his hands and kissed her "If you want we can go somewhere else instead of my mother's house."

"No, I am fine. I can go and meet your mother." Ishtar said while William smiled and said happily "Thanks, she will be so happy to meet you." William said then they got into the car and drove to his mother's again. After few minutes they arrived the house. William parked the car in long driving way in front of the house. Ishtar sighed and took deep breath then she got out of car. Ishtar held William's hand and started climbing the stairs. Every step she climbed, Ishtar sighed.

"Are you okay?"

"No, I am not."

"I asked you earlier and you said that you are alright."

"I was but now I am very nervous."

William held her hand tightly and said kindly "You will be okay. Whenever you want to leave, you can just tell me." Ishtar smiled and nodded her head

She breathed out deeply when William opened the door. They walked in a long aisle which has pictures on the wall and antiques things on every corner. Ishtar was looking on the pictures and searching for William then a dog started barking on them while another one ran into William, who got down and started playing with the dog

"William!" a woman voice said

"When did you adopt another puppy?" William asked

"Jessica did." Then she walked toward Ishtar and said "hey I am Margaret, William's mother." Willliam said immediately while he still caring the puppy "This is my girlfriend Ishtar."

His mother smiled then she hugged Ishtar with a big smile. They walked together to the living room. They were watching television. As soon as they got into the room, everyone stared at Ishtar, who her eyes moved quickly from one person to other to see their reaction, but everyone was silent.

"This is William's girlfriend." William's mother announced then she started intruduing her to her family while Ishtar started looking at each one and smiling.

"This is my daughter Jessica and her fiancé, Mike." Margaret pointed on a girl, who was sitting between two men, one of them was sitting on her right side and his left hand was on her shoulders "This is my youngest child Martin." Margaret pointed on a man who was, sitting beside Jessica on her left side

"This is my husband Jeff." Margaret pointed on a man, who was sitting alone.

Ishtar kept smiling while William released the puppy and let it to go down and held Ishtar's right hand and sat beside his sister. Immediately, his brother moved quickly from his place.

"You are squeezing me. " Jessica said to William

"Find for yourself another place." William said

"Why don't you find another place? I sat here before you."

William opened his legs widely "Move to another place."

"You have to move." Jessica said

"I like this spot." William said while Jessica seemed angry

"We will eat soon." Margaret said then she walked to the next room Ishtar tracked her in her eyes. Then Ishtar looked around her. The room were sitting on, it was big and also opened to another room was big and she considered it as the dinning room, because she saw a housekeeper was working there and Margaret was helping and talking to her. She looked up at the ceiling, which was high and several big shinning chandeliers were hanging there. The room, which they were sitting in, has a glass door which opens to the garden. Then she looked around the people around her and she felt she still nervous and anxious

"I am not hungry." Ishtar whispered in William's ear

William whisperd in her ear "You have to sit beside me. There is already chair for you."

"Okay."

"Does your girlfriend need something?" Margaret asked when she was coming back and looking at them

"She wants to go washroom." William said while Ishtar looked at him in disbeliefe

"Oh, yea. You can come with me." William's mother said

Ishtar looked disappointed then she stood up and walked with Margaret

"I am so happy that I finally met you." Margaret said to Ishtar

Ishtar smiled "Thanks."

"I have been waiting for you for a long time." Ishtar looked at her and kept smiling then after seconds of silent Margaret said kindly "You do not have to be shy dear. You can tell me what ever you want."

Ishtar looked at her "Okay."

"There is a chair for you. It has been sitting there for a long time."

Ishtar smiled "I know William told me."

William's mother smiled then she stopped and pointed on a door in front of her "Here is the washroom."

Ishtar sigh a relief then she got into washroom immediately. She sat on the bathroom carbet and started talking to herself "I should not come here....so stupid.....I should say I want go home." She stayed there for over five minutes then she took deep breath and got out

"Is everything fine?" Margaret asked Ishtar as soon as she saw her

"Yes." Then Ishtar said herself "I can not believe she was counting the minutes that I was in a washroom."

"You are very pale." Margaret said while Ishtar rubbed her face in her hands and walked quickly and sat beside William. After few minutes a housekeeper came and spoke to Margaret, who announced "food is ready."

William held Ishtar's left hand and walked together to the dinning room. As soon as they reached the big table, William pulled a chair for Ishtar and then he sat beside her. They sat beside Margaret and her husband on the right side of the table while Jessica and her fiancé and her brother sat opposite them.

"Where did you meet each other?" Margaret asked Ishtar and William, when they started eating

"We met in a bar." William said

"A bar!" Jessica said

"I work in the bar." Ishtar said

"What do you do?"

"I am a waiterss but I have another job because this is not enough for my rent and grocery and my mother's medications."

"Is your mother sick?" Margaret asked

"Yes, she is."

"I am so sorry." Margaret said kindly while Ishtar felt comfortable and relief. Margaret was so nice to Ishtar. She really was happy and showed to Ishtar, her desirable of seeing her. She is really an amazing woman.

"What is your another job."

"I work in a library." Ishtar said

"Oh, I guess you love book."

"Yes, i do."

Aftar few second of silence, William asked Jessica "When are you going to get married?"

"No specific date." She replied

"Why?" Margaret asked

"There is no plan."

"You have been engaged for a while and knowing each other for long time." Margaret seemed disappointed

"I do not know." Jessica said

"Next month we will travel to Hawaii for two week." Jessica's fiance said "Why don't you come with us? We will enjoy together."

Jessica seemed unhappy while Ishtar said quickly "Sorry, I can not. My mom is so sick and I can not leave her alone."

"Your sister is with her." William said

"She is busy with her fiancé." Ishtar explained

"Okay, I guess you will travel alone." William said then he asked "What did you name the new dog?"

"Coco." Margaret said

"Does the dogs like each other?"

"At beginning they barked at each other a lot, but now every thing is okay."

At that moment Ishtar kicked William's right foot. William looked at her strangely and then whispered in her left ear "What?"

Ishtar approached from him and covered her mouth "Did you finish eating?"

"Yes, I had done."

"Can we leave the table, please?"

"Yes." William said to Ishtar then he stood up then Ishtar stood beside him

"You finished eating." Margaret said

"Yes." William said then he held Ishtar's hand walked to living room with her

After few more minutes Jessica, her finace and her brother followed them.

"I want to watch." Jessica said

"I am not interested in watching your shows which starts since I bear until now." William, who was sitting on a couch and Ishtar sitting beside him, said while Jessica looked upset at him

"It is a new show." Jessica, who was trying to get the remote control from William's hand, said while William could not careless.

"Which episode is this one...... one hundred?" William said while Ishtar smiled

"No, five hundreds." Jessica said then she stood in front of him and her hands on her hips "i guess you watched this show with your girlfriend." She added

"We have never watched television together. This is the first time." Ishtar announced

"Can you move, please?" William said to his sister who was standing infront of him "I want to watch basketball."

"And I want to watch my show." Jessica said then her phone rang

"You can watch it in different room." William said

"Why don't you watch your game in different room?" Jessica said while her phone kept ringing

"We all want to watch the match." William said then he looked at them and added "And you are the only one, who wants to watch your show and answer your annoying phone."

Jessica looked sadly then she looked at her phone "It is Julia." She said while she was living the room and carrying Coco in her hands "Enjoy watching your basketball."

"Enjoy talking to your best friend." William said

"Julia said "hi" to you." Jessica said when she was on the phone while William looked at Ishtar and smiled

"Who is Julia?" Ishtar asked

"She is jessica's best friend." William said then he fouced on the match. After fifteen minutes, Ishtar felt uncomfortable and upset, while William kept whatcing the match and cheering during the game. She looked at William and whispered "Can we go out side?"

William looked at her and asked "Why?"

"I want to leave the room."

"As soon as this game will finish, we will leave." William said while he was looking at the television

"Let go now, please." Ishtar begged

"Few more minutes and the game will end." William held her right hand and kissed her lips while Ishtar said "Okay, fine."

William was busy watching basketball game. He was cheering and screaming and clapping with his brother, his step-father, and his sister's fiancé for their favourite team. He totally forgot about Ishtar, who was so bored.

"Let's leave." Ishtar begged again when it was break quarter

"The game did not finish, yet."

"But i want to leave."

"Soon, we will."

Ishtar was so sad and looked distracted. After few minutes William left the room and went to the washroom. Ishtar lowered her face and closed her eyes. Her left hand was on the edge of sofa while her left hand was rubbing her chin. Ishtar trembled when she felt there is a hand on her left shoulder.

"Are you okay?" the voice was very kind and smooth. Ishtar looked up and saw Margaret, looking at her and smiling.

Ishtar smiled then she said "I have a headache."

"I will bring you a pill." William said when he came back and heard Ishtar's words.

Ishtar held William's left hand in her both hands and said "I prefer going out side….. To the garden, please?"

William looked on a television then looked at Ishtar and sighed while Ishtar got up and whispered "If you want to keep watching I can go alone."

"It is cold outside."

"I will be fine."

"Do not worry, I am coming with you." William said while Ishtar walked to the garden house before him. As soon as she found hammocks, she ran to them while William was behind her. There were two hammocks in the garden house. One was small fit for one person and the second one was for two people. Ishtar chose the one that fit only for one. William stretched his left hand to her when he stood beside her and said "Are you feeling better now?"

"Yes, I do." Ishrar said happily

"Let go to the biger one." William said while he was pointing on the biger hammack

"I prefer this one. If you want, you can go alone." Ishtar ignored his stretched hand while

William turned his back to her and said "I am going inside again; if you want you can join me."

"Are you serious?" Ishtar looked at him and asked

William, who was walking far from her, said "Yes, I am."

"Okay go ahead. I will stay alone here." Ishtar yelled while William kept walking. Ishtar looked at him in disbelieve then she stood up as fast as she can and ran toward William and held his right hand "Where are you going?"

"Back inside the house."

"Why did you come from beginging?"

"I do not know."

"Okay go back inside and watch the game."

"I am."

Both were yelling on each other

"I can not believe you did that. You got one red flag." Ishtar said when William started walking back to the house

William stopped and looked at her then he said "What?"

"You got the first red flag."

"What is that mean?" William said while he was approaching from her

"Every time you treat me disrespectfully you will get red flag."

"When did I disrespect you?" William was unhappy and disappointed

"You preferred watching game over spending time with me in the house and now you want to leave me alone to go back to you bascketball game."

"I asked you to join me at big hammack but you refused."

"I said I want the small one while you can be on the big one."

William was disappointed. He sighed and controlled his temper and asked "how many flag did I get now?"

"Only one."

"How many am I allowed to have?"

"Three or four."

"Then you break up with me."

Ishtar looked at him "I will never break up with you."

William looked surprise "So what do flags mean?"

Ishtar hesitated before saying "Just warning."

"Warning! just like you did now."

"Yes, I did not warn you."

"And then everyone has individual path."

"No."

William looked unhappy at her. He was angry then he started counting on his hands after a deep breath "we have been going out since last year. We have no physical contact. We only shared few kisses. You want me to be part of your sister's wedding and help her to find the dress."

"I only ask you to drive me." Ishtar yelled

"I do not want." William yelled

"I only ask you. You do not have to come with us." Ishtar's voice was louder than before

"I do not want to go." William screamed

"Okay fine and for physical relationship you know from beginging i am virgin and i am saving myself until wedding day."

"I know that bu i choose to be with you."

"You do not have to." Ishtar yelled

"I want to." William screamed

"Why do you want to?" Ishtra screamed as well

"Becuase..."

"Becuase of what?"

"Because I love you." William confessed

"I love you too." Ishtar replied

They looked at each other smiling then William held her face and kissed Ishtar passionately. This was the first time they confessed to each other about their feeling

"I was going to tell you about my feeling since we were in the restaurant while we were dancing, but I hesitated." Ishtar confessed

"Why did not you say it?" William asked while he was still holding Ishtar's face in his hands

"I was not sure about your feeling." Ishtar said

"How?" William asked

"I decide to keep them for myself until you say it first."

"So if I do not say, you will never say me."

"Yea." Ishtar said then she smiled while William smiled then he kissed her again "Always tell me what is in your mind."

Ishtar smiled and said happily "sure."

William held her left hand and walked to big hammock. He lied down on the hammock then he pulled Ishtar toward him.

After few minutes Ishtar, who was close to the edge said "I am almost falling down, please make me room."

"This hammock is so big and it fit both of us but you keep complaing." William said while Ishtar was trying to get rid of him by pushing him by her right hand

"Move, please." She said

William sighed then he moved while he was saying "Can we go inside?"

"No, I want to stay here."

"Why?"

"I do not think your sister like me."

"My sister!" William was surprise

"Yes."

"Why do you care about my sister?" William said while Ishtar said nothing then he added "before we came her I said my mother wants to see you." William stopped "I did not say my sister." William stood up and looked at Ishtar smiling "My mother like you."

Ishtar smiled "I know. She is lovely person."

"She is the only person that you have to care about. " Ishtar nodded her head while William asked while he was extending his left hand to Ishtar "Can we back inside, please?"

"Why?"

"We suppose to be inside not here alone."

"I am happy here."

"Please!" William begged

Ishtar held his hand then she stood up and walked together toward the house

"It will be very normal for you when we come again here." William said

Ishtar looked surprise "Again!"

"Yes, my mother will be happy when she will see you again." William looked at Ishtar and added "You are my girlfriend."

Ishtar smiled then she said "Can we move quickly I am cold."

"You chose to come here."

"I know but I was bored at home." Ishtar said then she asked him when they got into the house "Are you going to watch the match again?"

"Yes."

"So when I will go home."

"Soon." William said then he entered the room and joined the rest to watch the game while Ishtar sat beside him

Chapter Five

THE CHOICE

Days passed Ishtar and William continued seeing each other. It was first Sunday of spring; William was out of town thus Ishtar decided to stay home with her sister and her fiancé and helped them planning for their wedding

"Ishtar can you come her, please?" her sister screamed while Ishtar was in the kitcken

"What's wrong?" Ishtar asked when she joined them and holding her cup of coffee

"He is saying we will get married as soon as possible."

Ishtar was shock "Why?"

"I have to leave the city. I find another job in different city with very good payment." The fiancé explained

"Your job is good here."

"It will be better there."

"I want …. But… I need to prepare myself." Ishtar's sister said while Ishtar looked at her and said angry "What do you mean by you want?"

"I mean I can marry any time."

"You have to leave the city." Ishtar said

"No, I am not leaving the city." Ishtar's sisiter said

"It will be contrated for two years." He said

"She is not leaving us." Ishtar said

The fiancé sighed "Okay I will think about it."

"You have to cancel it." Ishtar said

"Yes, you have and I will start looking here for an apartment to move in after getting married." Ishtar's sister said

"We will see some wedding dresses later." Ishtar said

"Oh yea. It is a good idea." Ishtar's sister said

"Can you leave us alone, please?" the fiance said angry while Ishtar looked at hin unhappy then she walked to the kitchen. She set her cup inside the sink and left the kitchen then she walked toward her room and looked rapily at her sister. She got her jacket, a book and got out of the room. She walked silently toward the front door and left the apartment unhappy. Ishtar inhaled the fresh air and started walking happily. As soon as she found a park, she got into and started walking. It was a big park. It has soccer, tennis, and basketball area. There were few kids playing soccer while other were with their mothers playing in playground. She walked for five minutes then she sat on a bench and started reading her book. After few minutes she put her book away and started watching the kids. Later William called her and said he wanted to see her. Ishtar was surprise and gave him the address. After a half an hour William was parking his car, and walked into the park but he could not find Ishtar. He sat on a bench and started looking at kids who were playing. After few minutes Ishtar, who was waiting for William, left her spot and started walking. Then she started smiling when she saw William's back. She walked as fast as she could toward him.

"I thought you are not coming any more." Ishtar said while her right hand was on William's left shoulder

William looked up "You changed your hair colour." William was surprise "No wonder I could not find you."

Ishtar looked surprised and confused at him. She changed her hair colour from black to red few days ago

"You were not able to find me." Ishtar said

"Yes, because of your hair colour."

"You are joking, right!"

"No, I am not." William said while Ishtar sighed "When did you change it?"

"Recently?" Ishtar said then she touched her hair "Do you like it?"

"Yes, I do." He said with a smile while Ishtar sat beside him and said "I did not know you are in town."

"I was supposed to stay longer because I want to buy my younger brother a car but my mother said after graduation he can have a car."

Ishtar smiled "I thought you had business meeting."

"Yea, I had meeting also." William said then he asked "How is your day so far?"

"I had an arguement with my sister's fiancé before I came here."

"Why?"

"He wants to marry and move to another city."

"Why did you argue with him?" William was confused

"I want my sister to live near me after marriage."

William looked at her "What did your sister choose?"

"They were discussing of moving when I left them."

"You can not force her to stay if she wants to move."

"I know I can not but i can tell her I will miss her alot if she moves."

William sighed then he looked at her right side. He asked when he saw a book "What are you reading?"

"It is a biography book." Ishtar said then she held the book and started flipping the pages

"What is that inside it?" William asked when he notice dry leaves

"You remember the flowers that you gave me on Valentine's Day."

"Yes."

Ishtar said happily "I have one of your flowers inside the book."

William was surprised "What?How?"

"I left it to dry then I used as a book mark."

"You threw the rest, did you?"

Ishtar smiled "Yes, I did."

"Why did you leave one of them?" William seemed confused

"It reminds me of you."

"Oh." Wiliam seemed happy then he looked at the sky and said "It is too sunny." He looked at Ishtar and asked "can we sit under a shade?"

"Yea, sure."

They walked for a minute then they sat on a grass in front of a tree. William sat on the grass first. His back was against the tree and his feet were bending, while Ishtar sat in front of him and her left hand was on William's left knee. They stayed silent for minutes then William asked "We will go to Patrick's son baptism, right?"

"I think yea."

"I will be the godfather." Ishtar looked surprise while William added "he asked me so I said yes, and my whole family will be there."

"Oh, I will see them again in the church."

"Actually we will meet them first in my mother's house."

"Why do we have to go there?"

"We will go together to the church."

Ishtar thought for seconds then she asked "The ceremony will be only in church, right!"

"No, we will go later to Patrick's house."

Ishtar sighed "I hope it will be only few people there."

"Maybe." William looked at her "You will be okay."

"I do not like meeting new people."

"You will be with me so you do not have to worry about new people."

Ishtar looked at him and said nothing while William said "let walk."

He stood up and helped Ishtar to stood up then they started walking beside each other

"What do i have to wear?" Ishtar was anxious

"You wear clothes."

Ishtar looked upset "I know I have to wear clother."

"So wear anything."

Ishtar looked at him "Can we go shopping?"

William looked at her "I hate shopping."

Ishtar stopped walking and said "I think I am not attending baptisim ceremony."

William stopped and looked at her then pulled her from her right hand and started walking again "You can go with your sister."

"Maybe she does not want to come with me. She was with her fiancé when I left the apartment."

"You can ask her."

"Or you can come with me."

William sighed then he asked when they passed beside the kids who were playing in the park in roder to change the subject of the conversation "I guess you like kids."

"Yea, I do. I spend hours with them weekly."

William pulled Ishtar at him. His left hand was holding her right hand, while his right hand was behind her back and kissed her

"Can we leave now, please?" Ishtar, who was upset, said

William sighed "Why?"

"I want to go shopping."

"Go later with your sister."

"Okay ...you can go to the baptisem without me."

"Why do I have to do everything you want?" William released Ishtar and seemed angry

"Oh, really." Ishtar seemed angery and upset "i thought we already discuss this."

William said nothing while Ishtar kept calm and said wormly "You have a choice. You can tell me later what your choice is."

At that moment, a kid walked toward them to take his soccer ball after it had been thrown from other kids while they were playing soccer. Ishtar looked at him while the kid was looking at them and other kids screaming on him. The distance that was between them and the kid was only one meter. Ishtar smiled while the kid said "Can I get my ball back, please?"

Ishtar looked at the ball then she kicked it back to the kid, whom looked at her with anger then he ran back to his friends holding his ball in his hands.

"I think the kid said himself when he saw us arguing threw the ball to me instead of yelling at each other." Ishtar, who was looking at the kid, said to William

William thought for seconds then he said "Why do you think he said that?"

"He seemed upset and angry."

"He only came to take the ball."

"And we did not throw it to him." Ishtar said while William, who was distracted, said nothing then she added while she was looking at the kids "I hope this kid will never visit the library which I work."

"Why?"

"What will I say to him if he tells me in front of the kids at story time that he saw you at the park arguing with a man?"

William looked at her "You mean your boyfriend."

Ishtar looked at him then she said while she started walking "I want to go back home."

William looked sadly at her then he walked beside her. Most of time, William was walking and his head down while Ishtar was looking rapidly at him from time to time. They kept silent until they reached Ishtar's apartment.

"What are you doing here?" Ishtar asked her sister when she saw her standing infront of the building

"I was so bored and alone at home so I came here."

"And my mother!" Ishtar seemed worried

"She went to neighbor's house."

"Okay let's go inside." Ishtar said while her sister sighed then she said "again home. I was already at home."

"We can go shopping if you want." William, who was behind them, said

Ishtar looked surprise at him then she said "You had chosen."

"Yes, I did. I chose to go with you." William said while they were getting into the building then he added "Relationships are exhausted."

"Yes, they are." Ishtar's sister agreed "I just had an arguing with my fiancé."

"I guess today is national arguing day." William announced

Ishtar smiled then she looked at her sister and asked "What did your fiance's decide about his new job?"

"He agreed to stay here."

Ishtar breathed a sigh of relief and said while she was opening the apartment door "good news."

"Where are we going?" Ishtar's sister asked when they got into the apartment

"We will go shopping." Ishtar said then she told her sister "Go and tell my mother we are leaving the apartment while i will prepare myself."

Ishtar's sister nodded her head and left the apartment while Ishtar set her book on a table, got into her room and took her purse while William was and Ishtar's sister were waiting Ishtar beside the apartment door

"Leave." Ishtar said when she was walking toward her sister and her boyfreind then they got out the apartment and Ishtar locked the door. They walked together out of the bulding and headed to the mall

"How long will we stay in the mall?" William asked Ishtar when they got into the mall

"I do not know." Ishtar said then she got into the first store after she saw a dress wore by mannequin while her sister asked "Where are you going?"

"I am going to check the dress." Ishtar said while William and her sister followed her

"A dress is perfect for the occasion, right?" Ishtar said while they were looking at the dress

"Yes, it is." William said

"You can sit there on a chair beside the fitten room." Ishtar said to William while she was pointing on a chair

"Okay." William said then he walked toward the chair

"I think I found some dresses." Ishtar said to her sister and William while she was carrying two dresses in her hands and standing infront of the fitting room.

William, who was sitting on a chair while Ishtar's sister was standing beside him, looked at her then William said "Go and try one of them."

"Okay." Ishtar said then she got into the fitting room

"What do you think?" Ishtar asked when she got out of the fitting room and wearing a black long dress

"No." Both said

The second dress was a gray long dress William said when Ishtar came out "Are you going to a church? You look like a nun."

"What do I have to wear?" Ishtar seemed disappointed

"More coulerful and exposable dress." William said

"I will go and bring more clothes." Ishtar's sister said then she walked away from them.

After that Ishtar tried several dresses. Finally she agreed on a button front floral V-neck dress

"You should buy a short dress instead than a long one." Ishtar's sister said after they left the store

"I like those one." Ishtar said

"It is just perfect." William, who was holding Ishtar's hand, said happily

"Why did you stop?" Ishtar asked her sister, who stopped walking

"It is wedding dresses." Ishtar's sister said while she was pointing on a wedding dress's store

"I know they are wedding dresses." Ishtar was confused

"Can I try?"

"You are not marrying soon."

"I think we will marry in fall."

"What?" Ishtar was shock

"It is only a thought."

"Really."

"Yes, we just had this thought few hours ago, during the argement." Ishtar's sister said while Ishtar looked at her and said nothing

"Can we leave, please?" William said

"Can she try a dress, please?" Ishtar said to him

"Okay." William agreed while Ishtar and her sister got into the bridal store

"Which style sould I try?" Ishtar's sister asked when they were looking at plenty of wedding dresses

"Try this one." Ishtar said while she was looking at off shoulder mermaid dress with lace

Ishtar's sister held the tag price "It is expensive."

"Go and try now." Ishtar commanded

"Okay." Ishtar's sister said then she held the dress and got into the dressing room

"We are not going to stay here for long, right?" William whispered to Ishtar while they were standing infront of the fitting room

Ishtar looked at him "No. Only four or five dress she is going to try."

William sighed then he sat on a chair while Ishtar looked at him and said "I know you hated shopping. As soon as we done we will leave."

"Thanks." William said kindly

"Another dress please," Ishtar's sister yelled from a changing room

"Let see the first one."

"No, I did not like it."

"Okay." Ishtar said then she went back to the dresses

"I am coming with you." William said while he was walking behind her

After they walked together Ishtar liked two dresses. She got one and gave the second to William, whom whispered when he held one of the dresses "I hope those are the last."

Ishtar thought for seconds "It will be if I try one of them."

"What?" William was surprise "Why?"

She stopped and looked at him "You want to leave the store early, right?"

"Yes."

"So I will try one of them."

"Okay." William agreed while Ishtar got into her sister changing room and gave her the dress then she got out and took the dress from William and got into the changing room. After few minutes Ishtar asked her sister "Are you ready?"

"Yes, I am." her sister replied then both got out of the room at same time and said "I do." Then they started laughing. William was distracted and fascinated by Ishtar's look. He stood up and walked toward her "You are stunning."

Ishtar looked at him "Thanks."

The dress was white long sleeveless, backless and v-neck

"I did not like it." Ishtar's sister announced then she got to the changing room again

Ishtar looked at William, whom held her left hand in his right hand and said "I like the dress."

"It is a wedding dress." Ishtar said then she released her hand from William's hand and got into the changing room again. As soon as they wore their clothes they left the mall.

"Why do you still have clothes here?" Julia asked Jessica while they were in Jessica's room at her mother's house

"Because this is my room."

"You do not live here."

"This is my room and it always will be." Jessica said then she added "In holidays I sleep here."

"Okay." Julia said

"Jessica, your brother and his girlfriend are in their way to here." William's mother announced while she was outside of her daughter's room

Jessica, who was sitting on a chair, walked toward the door and opened it then she said to her mother "Okay i will be ready soon."

"Okay, good." Her mother said then she walked away while Jessica closed the door and walked back to her chair

"She is coming with him. I can not believe that." Julia, who was beside Jessica, said sadly

"Of course they will be together. She is his girlfriend."

"I supposed to be with him." Julia said while she was standing up

Jessica looked surprise at her "What? I thought you have boyfriend."

"I broke up with him." Julia walked toward the mirror

"Why?"

"I do not like him. He is so boring." Julia said while she was standing infront of the mirror then she asked "Who is she?"

"You do not know her."

"How long do they have been together?" Julia said while she was walking toward Jessica

"I think six months." Jessica said

"They will break up soon."

"You already have been with him and it did not work."

"I should be different with him."

"What?" Jessica looked confused

Julia stood infront of the window and thought for seconds then she said "I will go to his apartment."

"What? Why?" Jessica was shocked then she walked toward her

"I want to meet her." Julia said

"She does not know you."

"She will."

"Why do you want to see her?"

"I do not know. I have not planned yet."

"Do not go there." Jessica said sharply

"I thought you love me."

"That is right, but I love my brother more than you."

"And you love me more than her."

"Just do not go."

"I will." Julia was serious

Jessica looked unhappy at her "he is happy with her."

"Maybe."

"You are wrong. She is the first who William brought to this house and he did not watch his favorite match so he can be with her."

"Okay, I will stay here until they will come in so I can meet her then I will leave."

"Why do you want to meet her?"

"Because I want to."

"Okay." Jessica said then she walked far from Julia

After few minutes William and Ishtar reached William's family house, William's mother was so excited to see them together. Then she called Jessica to come down so they can leave. Julia was the first one who came in

"Julia....." William's mother, who was surprise, said then she added "I did not know you still here."

"I am leaving." Julia smiled "I just want to say hello to William before I leave."

"He is with his girlfriend." William's mother said

"I know." Julia said then she ran toward William. She embraced him while saying "I missed you."

William released himself from her while Ishtar looked disappointed. He looked at Ishtar and said "This is my girlfriend, Ishtar."

"Hello, I am Julia."

Ishtar, who was jealous, she controlled her temper and said "Hello." Then she looked at William and said "can we leave now, please?"

"Yea, sure." William, who was holding Ishtar's left hand, said

"Nice to meet you, take care of William." Julia said before she left.

Ishtar looked at William and asked "what did she mean by take care of William?"

"I do not know." William said then he walked with Ishtar to the car.

The whole time on their way to the church Ishtar was silent and distracted when William tried to make a conversation with her. She answered in one word or two. Even seeing William being a godfather for a child and carrying him in his arms did not make Ishtar stop thinking in Julia and her words to her before she left.

"You have to tell me what is going on with you, please." William said Ishtar when they were sitting on a table in Patrick's house.

Ishtar looked at him and said "I am fine."

"No, you are not. You did not talk to me during the baptasim's ceremony or on our way to here."

"Who is she?" Ishtar asked

"Who?"

"The girl that I met in your mother's house."

"She is nobody."

"Did you date her?" Ishtar was angry

"No, I did not."

"Really!" Ishtar said quietly

"Yes." William said then he whispered "Can we talk about it later when we are alone."

"No."

"Why?"

"You have to be honest with me."

"I slept with her." William replied "Everything done since I met you." He added warmly

"It does not seem it was done for her." Ishtar said

William smiled "I do not care about her." then he asked after few seconds of silent "Are you jealous?"

"Yes, I am."

William smiled then he kissed her lips "You are the only person that I care about." Ishtar looked at him and said nothing while William said "I will bring you a cake." Ishtar smiled and nodded her head then she kept looking at William while he was walking far from her.

After few seconds Ishtar heard a voice from behind "How is your day going so far?"

Ishtar turned her face and looked at William's mother. She smiled and said "It is fine."

"I am sorry I heard part of your conversation with William." Ishtar looked at her sadly and said nothing while William's mother added "You have to know you are the only girl who William brought to home."

Ishtar smiled "I know."

William mother said "You do not have to care about Julia." Ishtar looked at her while William's mother added "She is only Jessica's best friend."

Ishtar looked at her then she said after seconds of thought "I always asked myself why William chooses me."

"You should ask him." Margaret said while she was looking at William, who was talking to Patrick's daughter

Ishtar looked at Margaret and smiled "Yea, I will."

"He is coming back." Margaret said then she added with a smile "You can ask him what ever you want."

"Thanks." Ishtar said while Margaret smiled then she walked far from her

"Can I ask you a question?" Ishtar asked when William was giving her a piece of cake

"Yes, sure."

"What was your thought about me when we first met at the bar?"

"Can you be specific?" William looked puzzeled

"Why did you want to date me?"

"Because I like you."

"Did you like me from first time you saw me?"

"No." Ishtar looked confused at him while William added "I was seeking for relationship."

"But my relationship with you is so different."

"Because there is no physical relationship."

"Yes."

William looked at her and said wormly "In the beginning it was very complicated and challenging for me being with a virgin woman and I did not like it but later ....something changed..."

"What happened?" Ishtar seemed excited and passionate

"Something inside me happened. Something pulled me to you. I like the challenge and I want to do it and I will keep doing it."

Ishtar looked at him "You like the challenge."

"Yes, I just want to be with you."

Ishtar felt happy then she kissed him.

"You did not eat your cake." William said to Ishtar when he saw her setting her cake plate aside and did not eat it

"I do not eat chochlate cake." She replied

"You should tell me." William stood up while Ishtar held his left hand and said "I do not want another cake." William looked at her while Ishtar added "Can you sit, please."

William asked while sitting "Do you have more questions?"

"Yes." Ishtar said then she asked "Why men are incapable to love?"

William thought for seconds "No, they are not."

"Yes, they are emotionless." Ishtar stopped then she added "You introduced the last girl you had been with by the girl you slept with."

"I think women say the same thing."

"No, we do not."

William looked at her "Maybe."

"Well when i met your family you introduced me as a girlfriend not a girl I am sleeping with."

"You are exceptional."

"I am not but men are unable to love."

William looked at her and said after seconds of thought "Okay, it is complicated to explain. Women invest too much in relationships while men not. For men relationships are mostly physically while women are mostly emotionally and we do not change easily. We do not give promises or hopes."

"Why?"

"I do not know." William stopped "Maybe because we have different body or the way girls educated when they are very young."

"You mean it is parents fault."

"Maybe, or it is just the body type as i said before."

"I did not agree."

"I can not say anything any more."

At that moment Patrick's daughter came back to William with another girl while

William smiled and said to Patrick's daughter "This is Ishtar. She is my girlfriend and she reads a story for kids in a library. I will leave you with her while i will talk to your father." William looked at Ishtar smiling then he said "enjoy you time with them." He stood up and walked far from them

"You read a story for the kids." Patrick's daughter said

"Yes, I do." Ishtar said

"Are they good stories?" she asked

"They are amazing stories."

"Can you give the address of the library to my mom, so we can see you there, please?" Patrick's daughter asked

"Of course I will." Ishtar said with a smile

"Are there many kids come to the library?" the other girl asked

"Every week there are new kids."

"Can we join them?"

"Sure you can any time."

At that time William came back "you can join us if you want." He said to Ishtar

"Yes, sure." Ishtar said happily then she got down and said to Patrick's daughter with a smile "I will give the address to your mother." Patrick's daughter smiled then William and Ishtar walked away from the girls

"Ishtar is not here?" Maria, who got into Ishtar's family apartment and her left hand on her stomach, said

"No, William has a baptism as a result she went with him." Ishtar's sister said

"Oh, I thought I will see her."

"I will tell her to come as fast as she can." Ishtar's sister said while Maria sat on a couch

"Why do you have all of those wedding dresses magazines?" Maria asked when she saw a pile of magazines on a table infront of her

"I am going to get married end of August." Ishtar's sister announced

"Wow, big news. You did not tell me before." Maria was surprise

"Nobody knows, except my mother."

"I know before Ishtar, don't I?" Maria said

"I do not see her. She is away all the time."

"She is always with her boyfriend. Is she not?"

"Yes, she is."

After minutes Ishtar came home. As soon as Maria saw her, she screamed "Finally, you are here."

Ishtar smiled then she asked while she was closing the apartment door "How are you Maria?"

"I am fine."

"And the baby?" Ishtar said while she was walking toward Maria

Maria rubbed her stomach and looked nervous "she is doing some movement...."

"She!" Ishtar and her sister said in same time before Maria finished her sentence

"Yea, I am having a girl."

"Are you excited?" Ishtar asked while she was sitting beside Maria

"Yes, I am. Your sister has news too."

Ishtar was surprised then she looked at her sister and asked "What is happening?"

"She is getting married." Maria said while she was pointing on Ishtar's sister

Ishtar looked at Maria "Who is getting married?"

"She is." Maria said while Ishtar looked at her sister sadly and waited for details "We have set a date." Her sister finally said

Ishtar said madly "You did not tell me."

"I barely see you."

"Oh yea and did not have a minute to tell me." Ishtar was angry

"I just told you."

"She just told me few minutes ago." Maria said while Ishtar looked at her and sighed then she asked her sister after minutes of silence "Did you find a dress?"

"I was looking for a dress before you came in."

"We can look together." Ishtar said kindly then her sister sat beside her and held magazines in her hands

"How is everything with William?" Maria asked

"Everything is perfect." Ishtar replied while she was looking at the magazine

"So you already had physical connection with him." Ishtar did not reply while Maria added "I guess you want to spend your entire life celibate?" Maria said

"This is my choice." Ishtar said after she threw the magazine on a table

Maria looked at her "He did not ask you anything or touched you."

"No."

"So he is not sexually attracted to you and you are a joke for him."

"What?" Ishtar was confused and surprised while Ishtar's sister listened carefully

"Yes."

"But he said he loves me."

"Okay you have to know losing your virginity is losing only few dots of blood." Maria said while Ishtar was listening carefully "If you want to lose it you should lose it for right person, not at right time. You should be in love with the person when you lose your virginity not when you signature a piece of paper."

Ishtar sighed and did not reply then she stood up and walked away from them while Maria said while she was looking disappointed at Ishtar "Okay walk away and say nothing."

"I want to go washroom." Ishtar said without looking at them. She was so frustrated on her sister and her bestfreind

Ishtar's sister stood up and walked away from Maria. After a minute Maria stood up and walked toward Ishtar's sister, whom was watching dresses on computer

"What do you take your engement ring off of your hand?" Maria asked Ishtar's sister when she looked at her hand after she sat beside her

"What?" Ishtar's sister said while looking at her fingers

"I do not know where I left it." Ishtar's sister said while she was standing up then she started looking at her engagement ring among the magazines.

"Check another place." Maria ordered when she noticed Ishtar's sister did not find the engagement ring.

"I will look around." Ishtar's sister said then she left the living room and headed to the kitchen and then washroom looking for the ring anxiously. When she did not see it, she came back to the living room. As soon as Maria saw her, she asked "Did you find it?"

"I searched in all the places that I went to but I could not find it." Ishtar's sister said sadly

"Ask your fiancé maybe you left the ring in his place." Maria said

"Yea. I will." Ishtar's sister said then she walked toward her room

"I can not believe you forgot your ring in the washroom." Ishtar yelled when she came to the living room and looking at her sister

Her sister looked at her and asked "I checked there."

"I got the washroom before you."

"Do you have it?"

"I am wearing."

"Really!" Her sister said happily while she was walking toward her sister then she added "It is big for your hand."

"It is amazing." Ishtar said when she was looking at the ring and smiling

"Give me the ring." Ishtar's sister said angry while Ishtar took the ring off of her finger then they walked toward Maria and they all sat on a couch to see the wedding dresses

"I like this one." Maria said when they saw a mermaid style dress.

"I tried it before and I did not like."

"Okay we can keep looking for more dresses." Maria said

"When did you know the gender of your baby?" Ishtar asked

"Last week." Then she announced "I am going to quit my job in the bar."

"What?" Ishtar was surprise "If you quit the job in a bar, I will do as well." Ishtar added

"I can not work any more. My morning sickness is not letting me to relax."

Ishtar looked at her surprise and stayed for second silence then she asked "Did you tell them that you will quit?"

"Yes, I said."

"When do you decide to leave the job?"

"End of next month." Maria said then she asked Ishtar's sister "How many people have you decide to have at your wedding?"

"Few, family and some friends."

"Where will the wedding take place?"

"I guess on a beach."

"Beach." Maria was surprised

"Yes, beach."

"Okay, it seemed romantic if you get the whole beach for yourself." Maria, who seemed unexcited, said

"You will be there, right?" Ishtar's sister said

"I do not know."

"Why?" Ishtar asked

Maria sighed then she asked "How long have you been together?"

"Over a year." Ishtar's sister replied

Maria stopped then she said "I need a dress."

"We all need a dress." Ishtar said

"We should all go together and look for dresses." Maria suggested

"Yea, we should all go." Ishtar said

Maria looked at Ishtar "You will come with us instead of going with your boyfriend, right!"

"Yes, I have many things to do."

"Okay, let's start next week." Maria said

"Okay, we will go next week." Ishtar said

Maria stood up "I am leaving now, I am so tired."

"Okay." Ishtar said then she stood up and walked with Maria to the door apartment

Chapter Six

THE BREAK UP

Spring passed and it was summer's day. Ishtar and William barely see each other now especially after Ishtar quit her job in the bar and most of the time she was busy with her sister and Maria. She was preparning for her sister wedding or helping Maria with her doctor's appointments

"You have to lose weight." The doctor said to Maria when she was in her clinic with Ishtar and Ishtar's sister visiting a doctor for check-up appointment "So you can avoid high pressure or sugar at delivering time."

"How much do I have to lose?"

"Around eight pound and you have to keep it until the due day."

Maria sighed "That is a lot."

"You still have two months. You have to lose the extra weight first then keep the weight until due day." The doctor said

"Okay I will try." Maria said

"You have to." The doctor said then she sat in her seat "You can leave now. Outside they will give you the date for next appointment."

Maria stood up then she got out of the room with Ishtar and her sister then they left the clinic after Maria got an appointment for the next visit.

"Do you think your child will be okay at delivery time?" Ishtar asked when they started walking in the same plaza

"She will be perfect."

"Do you think you can control your weight?"

"Yes, I can."

"Have you already picked a final name for your unborn daughter?" Ishtar's sister asked

"Maybe Emma or Ava." Then she said after seconds of silence "I do not think I will be able to attend the wedding."

Ishtar and her sister looked surprised and disappointed at her

"Why?" Ishtar asked

"My due day is before the wedding."

"You can come with your daughter."

"I do not know."

"You do not have to stay for so long there." Ishtar's sister said "You do not have to attend the ceremony at a church."

"You will marry at the church." Maria was surprise

"Yea I have to marry in the church." Ishtar's sister said

"My mother will not be happy if she skipped marrying at the church." Ishtar said

"Does she know about William?" Maria asked

"No, she does not." Ishtar said

"Of course she wants approval." Maria said

"No she does not. She prefers someone from our community." Ishtar's sister said then she added "We are never able to make her happy and satisfied."

"Well, we are just dating so she does not have to know." Ishtar said

Maria looked at her "Maybe you will marry him."

"Maybe." Ishtar seemed disappointed

"Is everything okay with him?" Maria asked

"I did not see him for a while since i quit my job at the bar and started spending time with you." Ishtar said sadly

Maria looked at her "When was the last time you saw him?"

"Last week."

"Do you speak with him on the phone?"

"Yea, I think last time was two days ago."

Maria stopped at looked at her "You should see him."

"Why?"

"You should have more connection with him."

Ishtar stopped then she looked at Maria "I think I will vistit him surprisingly at his apartment."

"Do you know the address?" Maria was surprise
"Yes, I do."
"I can drop there if you want." Maria suggested
Ishtar looked happy at her "Yes, I want."
"I am hungry." Ishtar's sister said
"I am craving on pizza." Maria said when they approached from pizza store
"Okay we will eat pizza." Ishtar said
"I will eat one slice only." Maria said
"Okay we will eat first then we will try some dresses." Ishtar suggested
They got into the pizza store and each one of them got their pizza slices and sat there to eat
"Do you want to see him tonight?" Maria asked Ishtar
"You mean William."
"Yes."
"Sure, we can go tonight to his apartment." Ishtae was excited
After few minutes Ishtar's sister said "Please, say you will attend my wedding."
"Yes, please. You will enjoy." Ishtar said while Maria did not respond
"I will take care of you and your daughter." Ishtar added
"You will be busy with your sister and your boyfriend."
"I do not think he will attend."
"You did invite him, right?"
"Yes, I did, but he did not confirm it yet." Ishtar said then she added after she looked at their empty plates "Okay, I guess we can try some dresses."
"Okay, let's go." Maria said then they stood up and walked to Maria's car. After less than fifteen minutes, they arrived to the wedding dresses store. The store was so big and it has over 50 dresses with different styles
"Wow, I like this store." Ishtar's sister said while she was looking at the dresses happily
"My cousin bought her dress from here. I hope you will find yours." Maria said to Ishtar's siter with a smile
"I guess she will find one." Ishtar said happily

"I will sit here and relax. I am so tired." Maria said while she was rubbing her stomach in her right hand and standing beside the chair

"Okay, I will find for her some dresses." Ishtar said then she walked far from Maria, who sat down on chair infront of changing room. After few minutes Ishtar and her sister came back to Maria with few dresses.

"Go and try them, we will be waiting here." Ishtar said when she stood beside Maria while her sister got into the room to try a dress. After few minutes Ishtar's sister got out of the room wearing ball gowns backless dress "I think I like this one." She announced happily

"You can try another one." Maria said

"But i like this one."

"We can hold for this one now but keep trying few more dresses then in the end you can decide." Maria suggested

Ishtar's sister smiled "Okay."

The second dress was off long dress "This is perfect for a wedding on the beach, right?" Ishtar said happily while she was looking at her sister

"Yes, it is perfet." Maria agreed

Ishtar's sister looked at both of them and said after she saw the happiness on their faces "Okay I will get this one." Then she got back inside the room to wear her clothes.

After they bought the dress and get out the store Maria said "Can we leave i am so tired?"

"Yea, we can." Ishtar said

"What is your feeling while your wedding date is approaching?" Maria asked Ishtar's sister when they got into the car

"I am excited and afraid at the same time."

"Why are you excited and afraid at same time?"

"It is marriage. Every thing is new." Ishtar's sister seemed angry

"Although it is new experience, you have to be just happy." Maria said

"I am happy."

"Why does she have to be happy?" Ishtar asked

"Why does she have to be afraid?" Maria said

"I guess she is just expecting a normal feeling."

"Being afraid is not part of marriage feeling."

"Yes, it is." Ishtar's sister said then she added sadly "And now I am terrified."

"Are you ready for marriage?" Maria asked

"I do not know." Ishtar's sister looked sad

"What do you mean by you do not know." Ishtar asked

"It is different life."

Ishtar, who seemed confused, said "Why don't you stay living with us then you can move slowly?"

"What do you mean?" her sister asked

"You can stay living with us in normal days then on weekend you can spend it in your new place with your fiancé." Ishtar said

"I do not think it is good idea." Ishtar's siter said

"Why?" Ishtar asked

"We already rented the apartment and one more month we will get the furniture, televisions and bed."

"You can think about it." Ishtar seemed unhappy

"Televisions! You only need one television." Maria said

"We need one for bedroom."

"Is it your fiance's idea?"

"Yes."

"Do not allow him to set a television in the bedroom." Maria suggested

"Why?"

"Your marriage later will be bored because you do not have communication with your husband." Maria said while Ishtar and her sister thought for moment then Maria added "He has to share the room only with you instead of ignoring you."

"I never thought of that." Ishtar's sister said

"How many bedrooms does the apartment have?"

"There are two."

"That is good. Incase if you will have big arguement with him, you can lock yourself in one of the rooms."

"You are frightening me."

"You have never lived with him and now you will move immediately and spend your whole day and night with him because you are marrying him." Maria looked at them but no one of them replied "Sorry but your mother's rules are so wrong." Both looked confused at her "staying virgin until the wedding day or moving with your man to his place after wedding day and marrying only from your community all of those rules are wrong and stupid."

"She did not tell me to stay virgin until my wedding day." Ishtar said

"She tought you since you were child no physical connection until wedding day then at wedding day you have to be sexually expert."

"I am the one who decide to stay virgin until wedding day."

"Because of her."

Ishtar looked at Maria then she said after minute of thinking "I think you are right."

"So you admit I am right." Ishtar did not reply "You change your mind about your virginity."

Ishtar looked at her "Maybe."

"Will you sleep with your boyfriend?"

"I do not know."

Maria smiled then she said "But you will think about it." Ishtar did not say a word.

Ishtar and her sister kept silent until they reached home

"We can relax for now then you can drop me at William's place." Ishtar said to Maria when they were infront of Ishtar's building

"Okay." Maria said while Ishtar and her sister got out of the car and got inside the building while Maria drove to her house.

"Do you think Maria is tough on us?" Ishtar's sister asked her when they got into their building

"No, she is not. She loves us and she is always right." Ishtar said then they got into the building and walked silently until they got into their apartment. Ishtar opened the door then she walked to her room. She walked to her bed and layed down in her bed looking at the ceiling while her sister left sat on a couch in the living room. After more than two hours Ishtar left her apartment after Maria called her. Ishtar got into the car and headed to William's apartment. It was 10.30 pm when they arrived at William's apartment

"Thanks." Ishtar said to Maria before she got out of the car

"You are going to sleep with him, are you not?"

"No."

"If you felt you are attractive to him physically, do not hesitate." Maria said while Ishtar sighed and did not respond then she said to Maria after seconds of silent "You can leave."

"Always remember what I told you." Maria said while Ishtar nodded her head and got out of the car

Ishtar was happy and anxious walking slowly to William's apartment. She got out of elevator and walked slowly to William's apartment then she stopped. She was shock when she found Julia in front of William's apartment. She stopped in her spot and looked at Julia. Julia's left foot was inside William's apartment while her right foot was out.

"I miss you." Julia said while William did not respond "I want to spend my night with you." Julia added then she moved her head and saw Ishtar. Julia smiled and looked back at William while Ishtar stepped backword then she ran to the elevator while William tried to get out and see what happened but Julia prevented him then she embraced him warmly and got into the apartment and closed the door.

As soon as Ishtar got out of the elevator she called Maria "Please, come in and take me." Her voice was deep and sad while her hand was shaken. After few minutes Maria arrived while Ishtar was behind of the building

"What happened?" Maria asked when Ishtar got into the car

"You were right i am a joke for him." Ishtar was angry

"Joke! What joke?"

"Can you drive?"

"Yah, sure." Maria started driving

"She was with him."

"Who?"

"His last woman."

"Did you talk to him?"

"No."

"Why?"

"He is not attractive to me sexually. You were right all the time. I am not enough for him. I am a joke for him." Ishtar was saying her words loudly and madly

"You choose to stay virgin until your wedding day."

"He never discussed with me my virginity."

"Not even once."

"Never."

Maria looked at Ishtar and said warmly "Do not worry you will be okay."

Ishtar looked sadly at her and did not respond.

At that night Ishtar was not able to sleep. She sometime cried other times she got angry on herself because she believed he loves her. Finally she slept at dawn time.

Next day was Friday; Ishtar woke up late and did not go to work. In the afternoon Maria was with her trying to comfort her.

"Do you want to go somewhere?" Maria asked kindly

"No, I just want to stay home."

"Did you talk to William?"

Ishtar looked angry at her "Why?"

"You have to discusse with him what happened."

"I do not want."

"You have to."

"I do not want to see him."

"Are you planning to take a break from him?"

Ishtar looked at her "Yea." She stood up "I want to get out of here."

"Do you want to walk?"

"Yea, I want to go for long walk."

Maria and Ishtar got out of the apartment and started walking to unknown place

"Can we eat ice cream?" Maria asked when they reached ice cream shop

"Of course we can." Ishtar said nicely then she got first into the ice cream shop. They bought their favorite ice cream then they got out of the shop

"I should ask the cashier if they are hiring." Ishtar said after they got out of the store

Maria looked at her and said "I did not know you are looking for another job."

"I was not but I need another job."

"You need money, right?"

"Yea, I need money and i have time."

"Your sister should spend her saving money on her wedding."

"She already chose a small wedding so she does not have too many expenses."

They started walking then Maria said after seconds of silence "Why does not your sister rent an apartment in your building?"

Ishtar looked at her "She was not able to find one at perfect time but we discussed this option and she will move to our building as soon as there is an available one."

"This is good so she can help you with your mother." Maria said while Ishtar smiled then Ishtar looked at her phone when it started ringing

"It is William, isn't?" Maria said

"Yes, it is him."

"Are you going to answer your phone?"

"No, I am not." Ishtar seemed careless

"You have to explain to him."

"I will."

"When?"

"I do not know." Ishtar was angry

Maria sighed and said "You have to know the truth so you can take the next step."

"What is the next step?"

"Staying with him or leaving him." Maria said sharply while Ishtar said nothing

They started walking in a big forest which was divided by a small river. There were few people in each side. Some of them were sitting, other running or riding a bicycle, and a few of them were walking. They walked into the bridge and crossed to the other side.

They walked silently for a while until they reach the end of other side then they crossed a tree and got into the park. There were few people there mostly mothers with their babies. They walked beside the swings. Ishtar stopped and grabbed one of them and sat on it then Maria followed her and sat on the second one. Then a mother came close to them and used another swing for her daughter.

Ishtar started moving backword and forward and the sadness on her face

"Do you think he loved me?" Ishtar asked

"Maybe he still loves you."

"Maybe not."

"Maybe he only was connected to you emotionally ....."

Before Maria finished her words Ishtar said "He never was connected to me."

"Maybe nothing happened between them." Maria said then she stood up while Ishtar looked at her and stood up.

After seconds of silence Ishtar said while they were walking "By the way i met the girl that she was in his apartment before."

Maria looked surprise at her and said "When! Where did you meet her?"

"In his mother's house." Maria said nothing while Ishtar added "When i met her he identified her by the girl who slept with. I guess he was always attracted to her sexually."

"So they had been together."

"Yea, and I was right about men." Ishtar stopped talking while Maria looked confused "They only care about their physical live and are unable to love." Ishtar said angry

"Of course they are capable of loving."

"Maybe, maybe not."

"They are. They love their kids and their partners." Maria said while Ishtar said nothing then Maria said "You have to call him and ask him about yesterday."

"I can not stop thinking about her."

"Your problem is him not her." Maria looked at her and she added "You prevent him from touching you."

"So you are blaming me on his action." Ishtar looked frustrated at her then she added "He chose to be with me. If he were unable to contuie, he can just tell me instead of spending with her his night behind my back."

"You have to tell him your decision."

"I break up with him."

"You still have to tell him you break up with him."

"I will if the phone rings again i am going to speak with him."

"Can we go home?" Maria stood up. She took a deep breathe then she added "I am so tired."

"Yes, sure." Ishtar said with a smile then they walked silently. After less than ten minutes

Ishtar's phone rang. Ishtar looked at Maria, whom ordered "Answr."

"I will." Ishtar said then she answered her phone

"Can I see you today?" William asked while Ishtar opened her mouth but there was no word coming out "Are you at home....." William asked

"I saw you last night with your girl." Ishtar said slowly while William stopped for seconds then he said "i am coimg to see you. I have to talk to you."

"You do not......" Ishtar did not add a word because William was already gone

"He is going to see you, is he not?" Maria said

"Yes, he is."

"Good."

Ishtar looked at her "But I do not want to talk to him."

Maria looked at her and said angry "You have to listen to him. Maybe for you it is over, but for him it is not." Maria was angry while Ishtar sighed and said nothing

When they reached Ishtar's apartment, Maria left Ishtar alone. William was outside of Ishtar's building. He tried to cuddle her, but Ishtar stopped him

"I have been waiting here for awhile." William said kindly

"What do you want?"

"Can we talk in different place?"

Ishtar stopped for second and looked at him "It is over between us." Ishtar opened the building door while William held her left hand "Nothing happened between us."

"She was in your apartment. I saw her."

William released her hand "We only kissed then ...."

"Enough." Ishtar was angry "You have to leave. I was a joke for you and I always will be a joke."

"You are not a joke."

"You never were sexually attracted to me."

"You want to stay virgin until your wedding day and I respect that."

"We never talked about my virginity."

"I thought you do not like talking about it."

"I do not believe you."

"Maria told....."

Ishtar looked angry and said loudly "You discussed with Maria my virginity but not me."

"I am so sorry."

"Leave." Ishtar was angry

"I did not do anything."

"I want to go."

"We are still okay, right?" William seemed helpless

"No, it is over." Ishtar said firmly

"You are mad now. I will consider it a small break."

Ishtar looked at him "You should go back to her." she walked away and left him alone. William looked sadly at her and left when Ishtar disappeared

"How long has it been since you broke up with William?" Maria asked Ishtar when they were shopping baby clothes for unborn daughter

"Over three weeks."

Maria looked at her "Did he try to get you back."

"Yes, he did. He mostly called me daily but we did not see each other." Ishtar sighed then she added while Maria looked at her "He asked me to consider it as red flag."

Maria looked at her and asked curiously "What did you say?"

"I said I do not know then he asked me to be only friends."

"What does he mean by friends?"

"He said if we eat in a restaurant I will pay my bill and if we decide to see a movie I will buy my ticket and popcorn."

"Eating in restaurant and watching movie." Maria said then she added after seconds of thought "I thought this is consider a date."

"This is what I told him. But he said we do not talk about romance and we can watch a documentary if we go to theater."

"Wow he planned for everything."

Ishtar smiled "He always does that."

Maria looked at her then she asked "What do you decide?"

"I missed him thus I agreed to be his friend."

Maria, who was holding a baby shoes, looked at her happily and asked "when will you meet him?"

"Next week."

"So it is a date."

"No." Ishtar said sharply

"So you are just friends now."

"Yes."

"Did you discuessed with him again the break up?"

"Not recently but he said before it was only a kiss."

"You have to trust him if you want to be with him again."

"We will only be friends."

Maria looked at her and walked toward her "You are still mad on him, are you not?"

"Yes, I am." Ishtar said

"But you still have feeling for him."

"Yes." Ishtar said while Maria smiled and went back to check the shoes again "I know you still in love with him."

"I never stop loving him."

"But you did not tell him."

Ishtar said nothing then she looked at two pair of shoes that Maria was holding "Are you going to buy them?"

"Yea, I think I need them."

"Does new born baby need shoes?"

Maria smiled "Yes, she does."

"By the way, I started working on ice cream store last Saturday." Ishtar said then she held baby shoes walking to the cashier

"Do you need it?"

"Yea, I am so bored at home and I told you I need money and it is near my apartment." Ishtar said then they stopped to purchase the baby shoes

"We have to go and check with a restaurant for baby shower." Maria said when they got into the car

"I told you I will help you if you do the baby shower at home."

"You can help me there also." Maria said then she added after seconds of thinking "I think I will have about 20 people on the baby shower."

"I thought they are less."

"Well they will be 20 including your mother, sister and you."

"Yea, I guess you need right. You need a bigger place than your house." Ishtar said

"I told you I need a restaurant." Maria said

"What did you buy so far?" Ishtar asked after few seconds of silence

Maria looked at her "Nothing. I will buy what I need after the baby shower."

At that moment Ishtar's phone rang

"Is William calling you?" Maria asked

"No. It is my sister." Ishtar seemed angry while Maria stayed silent until Ishtar finished her phone call

"What does she want?" Maria asked

"She needs a microwave oven."

"Are you going to purchase it today?"

"Yes, please."

"Okay we can go now if you want."

"I do not care if it is now or later."

"Are you planning to tell William you still have feeling for him?" Maria asked after few second of hesitation

Ishtar looked at her "I do not know."

"Do you think you can forgive him?"

"I do not know."

"Try to forgive him. He is your first love."

Ishtar looked at her and said after seconds of thought "I think I will."

Maria looked at her and crossed fingers while Ishtar smiled

Chapter Seven

THE PROPOSAL

On Sunday Ishtar's mother and sister went to a church while Ishtar dressed up early. She was very nervous and anxious. This was the first time seeing William since their break up. She wore a short yellow dress, short slevees with black ballet and black flat sandals. She sat on a couch and waited for him. After half an hour the door bell rang

"Happy birthday." William, who was holding a big bouquet of colorful flowers, said to Ishtar when she opened the door for him

"What?" Ishtar was surprised

"Oh," William was confused "I thought you told me before, your birthday is July 29."

"Oh, yea. July 29 is my birthday date. i just forget today is my birthday." Ishtar took the flowers with a smile while William looked happily at her

"I will come back." Ishtar said then she walked away from William

"Are you alone?" William asked while Ishtar was arranging the flowers in a vase

"Yea, they are in the church."

"You did not have plan for your birthday, did you?" William asked Ishtar when she joined him

"No, I did not."

"Can you spend it with me?" William said after few seconds of hesitation

"Yea, sure." Ishtar seemed happy then they walked together and got out of the apartment. They walked silently to the elevator then they got out of the building.They got into the car both of them and William started driving while Ishtar did not ask him about his direction

"How is your mother?" Ishtar asked after long silent

William looked at her then he said "i did not see her for long time."

"You did not even talk to her."

"Yea, I did. She asked me about you and I said she is fine."

"Oh." Ishtar figured out William did not tell his mother about their break up "Where are we going?" she asked while she was looking at the street

"We are going to celebrate your birthday." William said happily while Ishtar smiled

"Are we going to restaurant?" she asked

"No."

"So where we are going."

"It is surprise."

"Can I know the surprise, please?" Ishtar said while William looked lovely at her and said

"It is surprise."

"I already started to panic."

"We are cruising around the city."

"What?" Ishtar seemed surprise

William looked smiling "I hope you will like it."

"I am excited." Ishtar said while William parked his car. He got out of the car first then he opened the door for Ishtar while he was smiling. He held her left hand and walked quickly while Ishtar looked at her hand then she looked at him and said nothing. Then they walked toward a small yacht

"We are going to cruise in a yacht." William tried to comfort Ishtar when he noticed the surprise look on her face

"Okay." Ishtar said with a smile and walked silently with him. Then she got into the yacht and smiled to two men, who where waiting them. William held her right hand and helped her to get into the cabin.

"I guess you are hungry." William said when they sat on a table inside the cabin

"Yes, I am." Ishtar said happily

"But first we will celebrate your birthday." William said while Ishtar looked curious at him. After few seconds one of the men came in holding a small cake with lighted candles. William stood up and held the cake. He set the cake on a table while he was saying "Happy birthday."

Ishtar looked lovely at him and said "Thanks."

Ishtar blow the candles off happily then she cut her birthday cake and got one peice for her and one for William

"How have you been?" William asked while he was looking happily at her

"I am always busy with my sister and Maria." Ishtar said then she started eating from her birthday cake

William sighed then he asked "I mean how you coped during the night or free time when you are alone?"

"I just keep myself busy."

"I did not stop thinking about you." William said while Ishtar looked at him and said nothing

Then she said after minutes of silence "I have another job now."

William set away his plate after he finished eating his cake "I thought you do not want to work another job."

"I was trying to keep my mind fully occupied to avoid thinking about you." Ishtar looked at him and covered her mouth by her left hand. She regretted what she confessed

"I never stopped thinking about you." William said again "I still have feeling for you." William said while Ishtar kept herself busy with her cake

After a minute of silence William looked at Ishtar and asked "Do you need more cake?"

"No, thanks."

William stood up; he took the empty plates and the cake then he left the cabin while Ishtar looked through the window to the river. She knows she still loves him but she was afraid and confused about her life with him. She was afraid of not trusting him again.

"Let celebrate." William said when he came back with a bottle of champagne and two glasses followed by a man carrying plates of food. The man set the plates of food on a table and left while William set the galsses on a table and open the bottle.

"I hope you are happy." William said while he was pouring champagne for her

"I am." Ishtar said happily

"Today is going to be endless." William said happily then he sat while Ishtar looked at him and smiled then William added "You are going to see the whole city." William raised his glass and said happily "To your birthday."

Ishtar looked happily at him and said "I am so excited."

"I miss your smile." William said warmly while Ishtar sighed and said nothing then they kept silent for minutes while they were passing the Brooklyn Bridge

"What was your plan for today?"

"I did not know it was my birthday as I said so mostly I was going to wake up late, drink my coffee and spend my day with Maria or my sister and listen to them while they are complaining about their men." Ishtar said then she drank her whole glass of champagne while William looked surprised at her and said "You drank your whole glass."

"It is my birthday right?"

"Yes, it is."

"Can I get another drink?" Ishtar said while she was extending her right hand inorder to get more drink

"Sure you can." William said with a smile then he said while he was pouring more champagne for her "When I first met you, you were not drinking."

"Yea, I was not. Ishtar sighed then she added "I drank vodka shot with Maria's boyfriends last week."

William looked surprised "You did what!!"

"Well, she was complaining alot about our relationship so I had to do the shot to stop her."

"Complaining about us." William was curious

"Yea, she was telling me it was a mistake about breaking up with you."

"What did you say?"

Ishtar sighed "I said nothing. I just did the shot."

"Was she blaming you?"

Ishtar looked at him "Yes." Then she added with a smiled "Do you have vodka here?"

"Yes, I do." Then William said sharply "No shot for you today."

"Why?"

"You already had enough."

Ishtar looked unhappy then she sipped from her drink while William stood up and said "Go outside soon we will reach The Statue of Liberty."

Ishtar set her glass on a table and stood up "Okay."

William walked infront of her and got out of cabin then he extended his left hand for her and walked together then they stood beside each other looking at each other and smiling. Ishtar looked around her then she looked left and right. They were in the middle of The Statue of Liberty and the twin towers. She looked rapidly at the statue then at the towers then looked happily at William, who looked at her then he held her left hand and kissed it. He released her hand and pointed on the towers and said "My friend, Patrick works there. I saw him last week and told him it is over." William sighed "He is the only one that I told him we broke up." William stopped for seconds "My mother would be very disappointed if I tell her." William stopped and looked lovely at Ishtar then he held her both hands and said "The only woman, who I brought to my mother's house, is you."

Ishtar looked passionately at him while William held her hands tightly and asked after he took a deep breathe "will you be my girlfriend again?"

"Yes, I will." Ishtar said warmly and quickly

William's face shone while Ishtar smiled then he held her face in his both hands and kissed her then he looked at her and kissed her again.

"I love you." William said kindly

Ishtar smiled "I love you."

Wiliam looked at her and hugged her then he said while he was looking at the towers "Patrick will be happy if I told him we are back together."

"Are you planning to see him again?"

"Yes, maybe next week at his work." William brushed Ishtar's hair in his left hand and said "We can visit him together next time."

"Yes, sure." Ishtar said then she added after looking at The Statue of Liberty "Thanks for making my birthday so memorable."

William smiled "Thanks for being my girlfriend again." They gazed at each other then William said "after we got off the yacht we are going to my cottage." Ishtar looked puzzeled at him while William added "To continue celebrating your birthday."

"Okay." Ishtar said warmly

Then William held her hand and walked back to the cabin again "Can I tell you a secret?"

"Yes." Ishtar said

William sat on a chair and said "Maria called me after the break up and told me to never give up on you."

"What did you tell her?" Ishtar sat beside him

"I said I will never give up on you."

Ishtar smiled then she said after seconds of thinking "I guess it was before arguing with me about the break up."

William stood up and held Ishtar's hand and walked together inside the cabin then they sat together in a sofa "soon we will reach the cottage."

Ishtar smiled and said warmly "I miss being with you."

William kissed her forehead "we will always be together."

Ishtar sighed "Can I ask you something?"

"Yea, sure."

"Why did you let Julia to get into your apartment?"

William sighed "I do not know but you have to believe it was only a kiss." Ishtar sighed and turned her face away from him. After seconds of silence, William said kindly "You are the only woman that I want to be with." Ishtar looked at him while William said "You have to trust me."

"I am." Ishtar looked happily at him while William smiled and kissed her forhead.

As soon as they got off the yacht, Ishtar looked at the sky and smiled. She closed her eyes and inhaled the air. It was afternoon time and very sunny. William held her hand and walked together "Are you happy?" William asked with a smile

Ishtar looked at him "Yes."

"We almost reach the place." William said

Ishtar looked at him and smiled then she looked around her while they were infron of the cottage. On her left side there were two people infront of their cottage while on her right side there was a man sitting infront of his cottage and smoking. Before they got inside the cottage, William kissed her both hands and said sadly "I am sorry for hurting you."

123

Ishtar smiled "I considered it a red flag."

William smiled then he said "I accept that. Now please can you close your eyes and do not open them until I will tell you."

"What?" Ishtar was confused

"It is a surprise."

"I do not like surprises."

"My surprises are always good."

"Okay." Ishtar agreed and closed her eyes while William got a small scarf from his pocket

"You are getting more mysterious." Ishtar said to William when she saw the scarf in his hand

"It is a surprise as I said."

"Do I have to wear it?" Ishtar said when William was covering her eyes

"Yes." William replied while he was tying the scarf

William opened the door then he held Ishtar's right hand "I have to take my sandals off." Ishtar said before she stepped forward to got into the cottage

"I will take them off." William said then he got down on his knees while Ishtar raised her feet one by one so William can get rid of her shoes then he got off his shoes and closed the door. He held her right hand again and led her into the cottage.

Ishtar said after walking few steps "I am walking on something, right?"

William smiled "Yes, you are."

"I can feel and smell it."

"What do you feel or smell?" William asked

Ishtar stopped and rubbing her right foot by the ground and said "It is so smooth." Then she added "I guess the smell is coming from candels."

William smiled and said "Okay keep walking."

After few steps Ishtar stopped then she asked "Are they flowers?"

William smiled "Yes, they are."

"Am I walking on flowers?" Ishtar asked

William said "You can take the scarf off."

He released Ishtar's hand while Ishtar took the scarf off and opened her eyes. She was fasinated by the place. The place was very dark and all the curtains were closed.

She looked down and smiled. She was standing on flowers' leaves. She looked behind her and saw a big line of flowers' leaves started from the front door until the end of the room. She looked left and right, she noticed she was surrounded by heart-shape made from candles. Ishtar looked at William, who was standing beside her and smiling, and said "I did not know you are romantic."

William did not want to tell her the truth but he just got her back few hours ago. He has to be honest with her and got her trust back. He said after seconds of thoughts "I am not."

Ishtar looked surprise at him "What?"

"Actually Lisa did everything." Then William added when he saw the disappointed look on Ishtar's face "it was my idea but she organized."

Ishtar walked closed to him "Did she finish it while we were on a yacht?"

William smiled "Yes."

Ishtar smiled then she walked close to him "Thanks for everything."

William surrounded her waist by his arms while Ishtar asked when she was standing on her tip toes and smiling "Do I have to raise my feet every time when I want to kiss you?"

William smiled then he held her face in his hands and said "You do not have to. I can get down and kiss you."

Ishtar lowered her feet and looked happily at William, who kissed her then he picked her up. Ishtar looked panic at him and surrounded his neck by her both arms while William's arms were around her back. Ishtar smiled and kissed him

"Now we can reach each other without raising or lowering any parts of our body." William said then he smiled

"Yes, you are right." Ishtar said happily then they gazed at each other for seconds

"I love you." William said while Ishtar brushed his hair by her both hands then she looked at his lips and kissed him while William got her down and looked passionately at her. Ishtar sat on the flowers and started touching them while William was still standing and looking happily at her.

Ishtar looked at him and said "Thanks for everything."

William smiled then he said "I will bring a cake."

"A cake!" Ishtar was surprise then she said while she was standing "I already ate cake."

"This is from Patrick and Lisa." William said with a smile "Stay here, I will bring the cake." William said then he walked away

Ishtar looked at him then she sat again on flowers. After few minutes William brought a small cake with plates, knife, and forks.

William said kindly while he was sitting "Here is your second cake."

Ishtar smiled "thanks." Then she looked lovely at him and added "every thing is amazing with you."

"I will always be with you." William said warmly then he gave the knife to Ishtar, who cut a part from the cake and put it inside the plates. She gave one plate for William and kept one for her

"Happy birthday again." William said with a smile

"Thanks." Ishtar looked at him and said "I am so happy being with you again." William looked at her and smiled while Ishtar added "I guess in the end you are romantic."

"I will do my best although my freedom has limit with you."

"What?" Ishtar looked surprised at him

William looked at her "Yes, my freedom with you is so limited and I do not want to lose you again."

Ishtar looked sadly at him then she said "You have to be always honest and respectful."

William sighed then said kindly "I always will be." Then he looked at her empty plate "Do you want more cake or I can take it?"

"No, I am done with the cakes." Then Ishtar said after seconds of silent "Can I have a drink?"

"Sure you can it is your birthday." William said then he stood up and held the cake in his hands while Ishtar looked happily at him. When he came back, he was holding two glasses and bottle of wine. He gave the glasses to Ishtar, who set them beside her while William set the bottle of wine beside the glasses then he held the plates and forks in his left hand.

"I am coming back." William said then he walked toward the kitcken

"Where is the washroom?" Ishtar yelled while William was inside the kitcken.

William got out of the kitchen and pointed on his right side "In the end of this hallway."

"Okay." Ishtar said then she stood up and walked toward the washroom while William came back to their spot and waited for Ishtar. After few minutes Ishtar walked toward William happily. Before she sat William called her in her name. Ishtar looked at him and her jaw was dropped. She was looking at William while he was on one knee holding a ring in his hands "Will you marry me?" he asked

Ishtar was shock "What?"

"Will you marry me?" William said again happily

Ishtar looked happily at William, who was holding the ring in his hands and had gotten on one knee and proposed to her then she looked afraid at the ring and her face had changed while William was looking at her disappointed and confused. Ishtar took a deep breathe and looked at that man whom she loves and trust.

"Yes, I do." She said happily

William finally smiled while Ishtar extended her left arm straight out to him and looked happily at him. William looked at Ishtar's extended hand and sighed while he was dressing her the engagement ring. Ishtar looked at the ring and her heart beating was so fast while William held her hand and kissed it then he stood up while he was still holding her hand.

He looked at her and smiled then pulled her toward him while Ishtar looked smiling at him. "Thank for being my fiancée." He said then he kissed her

Ishtar looked lovely at him and said "I love you."

William smiled then he held her hand and sat. He opened the bottle of wine and poured in both glasses

Ishtar looked at the white gold ring and asked "Who bought the ring?"

"I did." William said while he was giving her the glass of wine

"Did Lisa help you?"

"I just ask her some questions but I bought the ring by myself." William said then he took a sip from his drink

"Does Maria know?"

"No?" William said

Ishtar looked surprise at him "Really! You always have conversations with her about me."

"Last time I spoke to her I think it was over a week ago and she told me not to let you go."

Ishtar looked at the ring "When did you decide to propose to me?"

William looked at her "When Julia visited me at my apartment, I realized you are the only one that i want to be with." Ishtar looked at him and did not know what to say while William asked her kindly "Did you like the ring?"

"Yes, I do."

"For a minute before you said I panicked."

"Yes, I was afraid but I want to be with you."

William looked lovely at her then he sat crossed- legs while Ishtar held her glass and started drinking

"Today you drink alot." William said while he was looking at her

Ishtar seemed unhappy "It is my birthday."

"Okay, it is your birthday so you can do whatever you want." William said then he added after few seconds of silence "Can we sit somewhere else."

Ishtar looked at him while she was drinking and nodded her head for agreement. William stood up then he carried the bottle of wine and his glass

"Can we sit outside?" Ishtar asked while she was standing

"Yea, sure we can." William said then they walked together to the front door of the cottage

Ishtar inhaled then she looked happily at the water while she was sitting on a chair beside William, who looked happily at her after he poured more wine for him

"Today you are engaged. In next birthday we will get married." William said after minutes of silent

Ishtar, who was holding her glass of wine, was shocked "What?"

William set his drink on a small table infront of him and looked at Ishtar "Is it too far? We can get married in Las vegas if you want."

"Vegas!" Ishtar was surprise. She set her glass of wine beside William's glass of wine and said "I do not want to get married in Vegas."

"It is legal and real. We will just visit one of the chapels there then we can get married."

"No, I do not want to get married there." Ishtar seemed angry

William looked at her and said warmly "You want to get married here, right?"

"Yes." Ishtar said then she added after seconds of thought "I do not know when I want to get married."

William looked at her "Those are only thought. Everything is able to change."

Ishtar sighed then she said "I think we can wait longer."

"You are afraid, are you not." William said then he stood up and kneeled in front of Ishtar and said while he was holding her both hands "I want hurt you again, I promise you. You do not have to be afraid."

Ishtar smiled "I know. I trust you."

William stood up and looked happily at her. He sighed then he returned back to his chair "How long do you want to wait until we can get married?" William asked

"I do not know." Ishtar said angry while William looked sadly at her then he said immediately "Do you like to visit my mother to tell her that we are engaged?"

"Yes." Ishtar seemed excited

"Okay." William stood up "I am going to blow out the candles and take a shower then we can leave."

"Okay." Ishtar said with a smile

William looked happily at her then he got his empty glass and got into the cottage. He turned the light on then he blew out the candles. He walked to the bathroom. He got his towel and got into the bathtub. After few minutes Ishtar took her glass and bottle of wine and got into the cottage. She walked to the kitcken. She set the bottle of wine on a table and drank the left of her wine. She thought for seconds then she set the empty glass beside the bottle. She left the kitchen and walked toward the bathroom. She opened the door while she was taking a deep breath. She looked at the shower spot and walked slowly to it.

"William!" she called him while she was standing beside the bathtub then she sighed while William turned off the shower faucet and got his head out of the shower curtain "Is everything okay?" he asked

"Can I come in?"

"What?" William was shock while Ishtar took her dress off then she stripped from her clothes and got into the shower while William, who said nothing, was looking at her in disbelief. She inhaled then she looked at William smiling "Turn on the shower faucet." She said while William looked at her from head to toe and sexual thoughts passed through his mind as he stood waiting for the shower to run warm enough for a bath. Ishtar closed her eyes while William looked at her tiny breast and rapidly look at her brown nipples

"Can you pass me the body wash, please?" Ishtar said while she was stepping more close from William "I need body wash." She whispered

William sighed "I am getting out of the shower it is all your."

Ishtar turned the shower faucet off and looked sadly at him and held his left hand "Why?"

William turned her back to her "Your body already turn me on. I can not stay here and keep watching you while you are taking a shower."

Ishtar held his arms and kissed his back "We can go later to the bedroom."

William, who was shock, looked at her and said "What?"

"I change my mind. I want to lose my virginity today." Ishtar said warmly

William held her face in his hands "I thought you want to wait until your wedding day."

"Yea, that was my plan but not any more." William kissed her lips and looked lovely at her while Ishtar added "I am so attractive sexually to you today."

William smiled then he said while he was kissing her face "I am always attracted to you."

"Maria said it is only few dots of blood." Ishtar said

William stopped kissed her then he said kindly "I had never slept with a virgin but I believe everything will be perfect."

"Now pass me the body wash, please?"

William held the bottle and said "I will rub your body." Before Ishtar said a word William squeeze big amout of body shower on her chest. Ishtar looked at her chest and smiled while William said "You have the most beautiful smile in the world. I felt so lonely and empty after you left me."

Ishtar looked sadly at him "I love you."

William kissed her then he rubbed the left side of her breast. Later he held her left nipple in his thumb and index finger for seconds then he started rubbing it by his thumb while Ishtar's chest was fast getting up and down. William looked at her then he turned to her right side and did the samething for her right nipple then he rubbed her stomach and turned her. He rubbed her back and pressed her butt then he moved his right hand between her legs

"I think we have to go to the bedroom." Ishtar suggested while William nodded his head for agreement then he turned the shower faucet on and washed their bodies while they were laughing. After cleaning their body William dried his body and her body then he turned the towel around his waist while he got out of the shower and passed the robe to Ishtar then he carried her and went to the bedroom. He got her down and started kissing her lips passionately and took off her robe while he dropped the towel from his waist. They were stripped infront of each other then William kissed her lips passionately while his right hand got down on her neck and started rubbing it then started kissing her neck while Ishtar's eyes were shinning. She was expecting a mixture feeling of joy and fear. He looked at her and rubbed her check while he was looking at her eyes. Ishtar climed into the bed and layed down on her back then William looked at her and crawled after her. He leaned over her then he got her nipples in his mouth one after another while Ishtar closed her eyes and was moaning under him then he got down to her stomach and kissed it. Ishtar opened her legs when William reached them. Then William kissed her forehead and said "Everything is going to be okay."

Finally after more than fifteen minutes, Ishtar lost her virginity. William kissed her forehead and layed down beside her

"Are you in pain?" William asked

"Yes, I am." Ishtar sighed then she said "I feel cold. I need warm clothes."

William stood up and chose clothes for her from his closet then he helped Ishtar to wear them then he wore his clothes.

"They are so big." Ishtar said while she was looking at the clothes while William smiled and led her to the bed. William layed down on his back then Ishtar layed beside him. Both were looking at the ceiling. Then William covered Ishtar and looked at her smiling and rubbing her right cheek happily. Ishtar looked at William then she flipped to her right side while William raised his head and kissed her forehead and her nose "Thanks for making me the happiest man in the world." He said kindly

Ishtar raised her head and kissed him "I love you."

William smiled then he layed on his back while Ishtar rested her head on his chest. William started brushing her hair and looking at the ceiling while Ishtar closed her eyes

"Everything happened so quickly today." Ishtar said

"What?" William said

"We got back together, and then I got engaged and lost my virginity." Ishtar stopped for second then she added "All it happened in my birthday."

"It is not quickly. We have been together since last year."

Ishtar smiled "I guess you are right."

"I am always right." William said while Ishtar smiled then she closed her eyes while William rubbed her stomach "How do you feel?"

"Better."

After minutes of thought William asked "Can you sleep here tonight?"

"Why?"

"Well you are my fiancee now and I believe it is time to sleep on one bed together then you can leave in the next day."

"Okay, I guess you are right."

"So you are going to sleep here tonight." William said happily

"I think I will stay."

William smiled happily then he asked after minutes of silent "Am I going to see you next week?"

"No."

"Why?"

"It is henna's night for my sister."

"What?"

"The ceremony happens during night time and mostly women are invited."

"Oh, you mean bachelorette party."

Ishtar thought for seconds then she said "But there are no stripers or drinks, we just stay at home with women who are invited then the groom to be come in with his relatives to bride's to be house. And later they dye groom's to be and bride's to be hands. After finishing Henna's ceremony, the relatives take clothes, make ups, shoes, and every thing that belongs to the bride to the groom's house."

"Okay, I can see you after that."

"Oh, I have to organize my sister clothes and items."

"You can organize them later."

"Okay, I will contact with you after cleaning."

"It only takes an hour to organize every thing." William said sadly then he said while he was raising her head "Shall we leave?" William got out of bed

Ishtar looked sadly at him and sighed "Why are you angry?" Ishtar asked

William looked at her "Because you are not making any effort to make this relationship works."

Ishtar moved toward to him "Why are saying that?"

"When we started dating I respected your belief to remain virgin until your wedding day. But, when you saw a woman infront of my apartment your broke up with me without even knowing the story."

"But I changed my beliefes for you."

"We just got engaged and I asked you to spend time with me but you prefer to be with some stranger woman instead of being with me."

Ishtar looked sadly at him "I guess now you want to break up with me."

William looked lovely at her "No, no." He held her face in his hand "I love you and I will never break up with you."

Ishtar looked at him and smiled "So it is a red flag for me."

William smiled "Yes." Then he asked "Do you still want to go to my mother's house?"

"Yea we can go but now I am hungry."

"Okay we will eat first then we can go to my mother's house."

"Okay, good." Ishtar agreed

William said happily "My mother will be overjoyed when she will see the ring on your finger."

"I am excited to see her."

"Okay, let's leave now." William said then he held Ishtar's right hand and got out of the cottage. After more than an hour William and Ishtar arrived in his mother's house, William held Ishtar's left hand and walked together toward the front door. William opened the door while his mother saw them when she was getting down the stairs.

"What an amazing surprise?" William's mother said

William and Ishtar looked at her smiling. She walked quickly toward Ishtar and hugged her "Let's go inside." Margaret said and walked with Ishtar while William followed them.

As soon as they reached the living room the dogs ran toward William, who kneeled on his knees and started rubbing them

"Are you alone?" William asked when he was looking around

"Yes, I am." Margaret and Ishtar sat on a couch beside each other "Jessica and her finace left half an hour ago." William stood up while his mother asked him "Why did you not come earlier?"

"We were in a cottage."

"Oh, you just came from there."

"Yea and we are going back there after we leave." William said while he was sitting on a chair while the dogs sat beside Margaret on a couch

"Okay, I am going to prepare dinner." Maragret said while she was standing up

"We ate before we came in." William said

"Do you need something?" Magaret looked at Ishtar and asked

"No, thank." Ishtar said with a smile

"We are engaged." William announced

"What?" Margaret, who was shocked, looked at William and asked "Are you joking?"

"No, I am not." William said

Magaret smiled happily and walked toward Ishtar and said while she was extending her hands "let me see your hand."

Ishtar responded to her and extended her hand happily while Margaret said "It is an engagement ring." She bent down and embraced Ishtar tightly "I can not belive you are engaged." Margaret said while she was looking at Ishtar happily then she said "congratulation."

"Thanks." Ishtar said with a smile

Margaret sat beside Ishtar and looked at William "Why did you not tell me?"

"I just proposed to her few hours ago." William said

Margaret sighed then she said "Finally you are going to get married." William smiled and did not respond "I hope the wedding will be soon and do not delay like Jessica."

"We have not planned yet?" Ishtar said

"Actually I want to be married next year but you did not accept." William said

"Why?" Margaret asked "You do not have to be engaged for years until you get married."

Ishtar looked at William then she said "No, we want."

"Will be a big or small wedding?"

William looked at Ishtar and said "I prefer small wedding."

Ishtar nodded her head "I prefer small also."

Margaret looked at Ishtar and smiled "Since the first time I saw you I felt you are the last woman in his life."

"Really!" Ishtar seemed surprise then she looked at William and later looked back at Margaret and said "We just had an argument before we came here."

"Yes we had. But you still my only woman and you always will be." William said happily while Ishtar said nothing

"From beginning you were the one. You were the first woman to sit beside him in this house." Margaret said

After seconds of silent Margaret said "why do not you go to your apartment instead of going to your cottage? Your cottage is out of city."

"I prefer the cottage over the apartment." Ishtar said

William looked at Ishtar "We will go to the cottage." Then he stood up and walked toward Ishtar while he was saying"We are leaving now."

"Can you stay longer?" William's mother asked while Ishtar stood up beside him

William said quickly while he was holding Ishtar's hands "No, we will leave."

Then William and Ishtar walked together to the front door while William's mother was walking beside them

Chapter Eight

DANCE FOR ME

On Saturday, august, 11, 2001 was Ishtar's sister wedding. They already married in the church days earlier and now it was a wedding ceremony which took place on a beach. The celebration started in the late afternoon and there were about 30 people attended the wedding.

"She is gorgeous. The most amazing bride I have ever seen." Maria said to Ishtar while they were looking at Ishtar's sister happily

"I know. She is stunning." Ishtar said happily

"I hope you will get married as fast as she did."

Ishtar looked at her "No, I need more time."

"No, you do not need more time."

"Yes, I need." Ishtar said firmly

"Is William going to attend the wedding?"

"I do not know."

"Why!"

"He is with his friend and they have a meeting with someone."

Maria looked at Ishtar from head to toes "I believe William will take you home after seeing you in this dress."

"Actually he asked me to spend my night with him in his apartment."

"Yes, it is very good idea." Maria was excited

"No, it is not."

"Why?"

Ishtar said after seconds of silence "Maybe we will spend the night at my apartment."

"Your mother is not going to allow you." Maria said while Ishtar looked sadly and did not respond then Maria added "You can spend time with him now instead of night time."

"He prefers his apartment and night time." Ishtar said while Maria seemed confused then Ishtar whispered "He wants us to be alone."

"Alone! Why?" Maria was curious

"Alone is better."

"I still can not understand why he wants to be alone with you while you do not share bed with him."

Ishtar sighed then she whispered after seconds of thought "I slept with him."

"What?" Maria, who was rubbing her stomack, said loudly while Ishtar looked angry at her then they both looked at people who were sitting beside them

"What happened?" Maria whispered

Ishtar said "I did what you always asked me to do."

"How?"

"I change my mind about sleeping with him."

"When did that happen?" Maria was happy

"In my birthday."

"How many times so far?" Maria was curious while Ishtar looked mad and did not respond "I said how many times." She repeated angry

Ishtar smiled "Three times."

"Three times and you did not tell me."

"I did not know how to tell you."

"Really!" Maria smiled then she added "I belive tonight it is going to be the fourth."

"Maybe."

"I will stay with your mother."

"You are already suffering from your delayed pragnancy."

"I will be fine."

"No, you will not."

"Can you at least think about it?"

"Okay, I will."

After more than an hour, the groom and the bride danced their first dance while Ishtar's cell phone rang. She stood up and walked far from Maria and people. After few minutes Ishtar came back to her spot beside Maria

"Is he coming?" Maria asked Ishtar

"Yes." Ishtar said while she was sitting

"He will be so fascinated when he will see you."

Ishtar looked at her and did not respond then she asked after seconds of thought "What is the perfect gift for a man at his birthday?"

"It is his first birthday with you, right?"

"Yes, it is."

"What did he give you on your birthday?"

Ishtar thought "We toured around newyork city then we got engaged."

Maria looked at her then she said after seconds of thought "You can cook for him."

"What else?"

"You can buy him a tie, perfume or a watch."

"I want something romantic."

"You can move to live with him."

"I can not leave my mother alone."

"You can move to William's building."

"I never thought of that."

"Because you are stupid."

Ishtar looked disappointed at Maria then she said "More ideas about birthday gifts, please."

"You can give him a mug and a picture of you with him printed on it."

"A mug!!" Ishtar was surprise

"Yes I did once but it was not the first birthday gift."

"No, I prefer to cook for him."

"You can cook for him his favourite meal and then you can eat together in the bed." Maria said happily

"Yea, I think I will cook." Ishtar said then she asked when she saw Maria rubbing her stomach and taking a deep breath "Are you okay?"

"I am in pain."

Ishtar touched Maria's stomack while she was asking "Do you want go to the hospital?"

Maria took a deep breathe again and said painfully "Can you stay beside me, please?"

Ishtar smiled "Yes, sure."

After few minutes Maria said "I am okay now. The pain had gone."

"Okay, good." Ishtar said happily then she looked at her phone when it started ringing

"Is William calling you?" Maria asked

"Yes, I think he is here I am leaving you now for minutes." Ishtar said while she was standing

"Sure." Maria said while Ishar started walking far from her to see William. As soon as she saw him, she moved slowly toward him. She waved in her right hand with a smile. William looked at her from head to toe and said warmly "You are gorgeous."

"Thanks."

Ishtar was wearing a blue satin dress with v- neck and blackless. The dress was a toe-length and has a high slit on her left side. Her hair was a bonytail. Her shoes were silver and high.

He stopped then he held her right hand by his right hand and asked her "can you turn around, please?"

Ishtar smiled then she did what he asked. She turned around herself twice then William released her right hand and held her from her waist by his both hands while Ishtar's hands were on his shoulders.

"I like your dress." William said then he held Ishtar's right hand and walked beside her "I do not mind to take it off." He whispered on her right ear

Ishtar smiled then she looked at him "We will sit beside Maria."

William smiled to Maria and sat beside her while Ishtar left them to talk to her sister while William kept watching her. After few minutes Ishtar came back to her spot

"When will the wedding end?" William asked Ishtar after she sat beside him

"Soon." Ishtar replied

"What did you decide about spending your rest of the day with me?" William asked

"I will take care of your mother." Maria said

"You can not take care of her." Ishtar said

"I can."

"Your mother does not need someone to take care of her for the whole night!" William said sadly while Ishtar looked at him

"I will stay with your mother." Maria said

"Okay, we will go together to the apartment then we will leave after my mother takes her medicine." Ishtar said

William looked happy "Okay, I agree."

Before the party ended Ishtar's sister decided to throw her bridal flowers. Ishtar and few women gathered to catch it. Unfortunately Ishtar did not catch the bridal flowers then she returned disappointed to William and Maria

"Why are you sad?" William asked Ishtar

"I want that bridal flowers." Ishtar said sadly while she was sitting beside him

"I believe if you were taller you could get it."

Ishtar looked unhappy at him and said "There are shorter women than me here."

"You are the shortest one and most beautiful woman in the world."

Ishtar smiled then she said "I still want that bridal flowers."

William asked "Why?"

"If I catch it, my wedding will be next."

"You are already engaged." William said while Ishtar did not respond then he added "I will marry you soon."

"I know."

"Why are you afraid?"

Ishtar thought for second "I think because I am superstitious."

William kissed her right hand "You just did not get it because you are short." Ishtar looked at him then she smiled

After less than half an hour William drove Ishtar, her mother and Maria to Ishtar's apartment. As soon as they reached the apartment, Maria had some pain as aresult William and Ishtar sat beside her while Ishtar's mother went to her room to rest after she took her medicine.

"You should go hospital." Ishtar said while she was standing up

William looked at Ishtar and asked "Where are you going?"

"I am going to change so we can take her to the hospital."

"I am fine the pain is on and off." Maria said then she took deep breathe "The pain will be gone soon just like what happened earlier in your sister's wedding." Maria said while she was holding Ishtar's left hand

"Do you want to go to the hospital now?" William asked Maria

"It is not the baby time yet." Maria said then she added while she was looking at Ishtar and holding her hand "The pain is gone. You can leave now. You do not have to change."

Ishtar looked at her "We will leave when you are okay."

"I am fine." Maria said firmly

Ishtar sat beside William then she said while she was turning the televation on "We can wait few more minutes."

"Is your sister going honeymoon somewhere?" William asked

"No." Ishtar said

Then William looked at the picture in the wall and asked "This is you when you were a child."

"Yes, it is my mother, sister and me."

"What are you wearing?"

"They are traditional clothes. We mostly wear them at a festival."

"What is that on your head?"

"It is a wreath of red flowers."

"Are they roses?"

"No, they are different flowers." Ishtar said while she was changing a channel

"Wait, wait" William said

Ishtar looked at William "What?"

"Go back to the dancer."

Maria stood up while Ishtar asked her "Are you alright?"

"Yea, I am. I am just going to the washroom." Maria replied

"Do you need help?"

"No." Maria said then she walked far from them

"Are you still okay Maria?" Ishtar asked Maria after she walked few steps

"Yes, I am."

"Do you need water?" Ishtar asked William while she was looking at him. William, who was looking very interested on the television, did not respond

Ishtar seemed disappointed and looked at the dancer who was performing on the televions. The dancer was wearing a belly dance custom which contained a bra and a skirt, both were in red colour. The bra has red beads hanging down of up to 7 inches in length. The beads were matched with the bra. The bottom was also a red chiffon skirt which has two thigh high slit. Around her neck there was a red belly dancing isis wings. The dancer was once shaking her shoulders other time doing the circles movement in her hips or hiding herself in the isis wings then exposing herself slowly. Ishtar looked at William and felt sad. He seemed distracted and enjoying her dancing while Ishtar was jealous and very disappointed.

She stood up and said angry "You are interested in her dancing, are you not?"

"Yes, I liked her dancing." William said without looking at her

"Why?"

William looked at her "Am I not allowed?"

"No, you are not." Ishtar said then she pulled her dress and opened her legs widely and sat on William's lap

William looked at her and said "You are blocking the t.v."

Ishtar surrounded William's neck by her arms "I am better dancer than her."

"Maybe." He said then he started rubbing her back by his left hand while his right hand was rubbing Ishtar's left leg. He looked at her and kissed her lips then he kissed her neck and her right shoulder

"Shall we go to the apartment?" he asked

Ishtar noded her head for agreement then she said while she was standing up "Let me check on Maria first."

"Okay." William said with a smile while Ishtar walked slowly to the washroom

"Do you need help?" Ishtar asked while she was knoching the washroom door

Maria opened the washroom door and said sadly "The pain is back again."

"You have to rest."

"The pain is stronger now." Maria said while they were walking slowly

Ishtar looked sadly at her and said "I guess you have to go to the hospital."

"Can you call Liam, please?" Maria said

"William can drive us to the hospital." Ishtar said while Maria nodded her head for agreement

"Is everything okay?" William asked when he saw Ishtar was helping Maria in her walking

"She has to go to the hospital." Ishtar said then she added "You have to drive us to the hospital."

"Okay." William said then he stood up

"Oh, no." Ishtar suddenly yelled

"What happened?" William asked

Ishtar looked at him "Her water broken."

"What?" William was puzzeled

"On my dress." Ishtar said while William looked at Maria and said nothing

Maria looked disappointed at William's face and said sadly"Sorry, I ruined the dress."

"It is okay." Ishtar said then she looked at William and said "Take her to the car while I will go and change my clothes and call her partner."

"Okay." William said then he held Maria and walked together then Maria looked at Ishtar and yelled "Call Liam, please?"

"Yes, I will."

"Tell him to bring the bag of clothes that is set beside the closet's door in our room."

"Okay." Ishtar said then she left them alone while Maria and William walked slowly to the apartment door

"I am sorry William for ruining your night." Maria said to William while they were in the elevator

William looked at her and smiled "It is fine."

"No it is not fine. I know you are upset."

William looked at her "I wished I had a dance with her in that dress but this is not important now. You have to be in the hospital and we have to walk faster." William said when they got out of the elevator and walked toward the car. After few minutes Ishtar followed them and got into the car

"Did you call Liam?" Maria asked Ishtar as soon as Ishtar sat beside her in the back seat of the car while William started driving

"Yes, I did."

"I am so afraid." Maria said after few minutes

"I am with you and soon we will be at the hospital."

"Can you drive faster?" Maria yelled "the pain is horrible.'

"Only few minutes left to reach the hospital." William announced

"The pain is different now." Maria said while William sighed and increased the speed.

"Do not worry soon we will see the doctors." Ishtar, who was looking sadly at her suffering friend, said

After less than five minutes they reached the hospital

"Liam is in his way to the hospital." Ishtar siad when they got off the car

Maria looked at them and said happily "Thank you." Then she sat on a chair while William went to talk to the nurse

She looked sadly at Ishtar and said "Sorry for ruining your dress and plan."

"You do not have to worry about me focus on yourself and your baby."

"As soon as Liam arrives, you can leave."

"I will decide when I can leave."

Maria looked at William then she looked at Ishtar "He seemed disappointed."

"He is concern." Ishtar said while she was looking at William

After few seconds William said to Maria when he came back "The nurse will come soon and take you."

"Thanks for everything." Maria said

William said with a smiled "You are welcome."

After less than half an hour Maria entered the labour room with her partner while Ishtar and William sat on chairs waiting for good news

"Sorry for ruining everything." Ishtar said sadly

William looked at her "It is fine but you can fix it."

"How?"

"On my birthday you can wear a dancer clothes."

"You mean what the dancer was wearing when you were watching the television."

"Yes."

"Okay, I can do that."

"This is will be your gift for my birthday."

"Ishtar looked at him "Okay, I think I can wear the costume."

William smiled "I am so excited for it." Then he said while he was holding Ishtar's right hand "Are we going to stay here."

"No." Ishtar stood up "we will go and buy flowers, balloons and food for Maria."

"Are we going to my apartment?" William asked while he was standing beside Ishtar

Ishtar looked at him "No, We have to be beside Maria."

"We will leave now."

"Yes, we have to buy the items and come back here." Ishtar said

William looked at her and said "Okay."

On August, 22 which is William's birthday, Ishtar finished her job at four o'clock in the afternoon then she went home to relax and cook for her mother. At evening time, she took a shower and changed her clothes. She wore green crossover neck empire maxi dress and took her gift bag. Before she left the apartment, she gave her mother the medicine and walked happily to the elevator then she got out of the building.

Ishtar looked happily at William, who was waiting her infront of his car outside the building and said happily to him "Happy birthday."

"Did you bring the gift?" William asked while he was opening the door for her

"Yes, it is in the bag." Ishtar replied while she was getting into the car

"Which colour is it?" William asked when he got into the car

"It is a gift. You have to wait to see it."

"I am so excited."

"I can not stay for so long."

William looked at her and said "Because of my mother."

"Yes."

"Soon this problem will be solved."

"What do you mean?" Ishtar was confused

"You have to move to my building so we can live together."

"What about my mother?"

"I already bought an apartment for you in my building."

"What?" Ishtar was surprised

"After the celebration of my birthday, we can see the apartment together."

"When did you buy it?"

"Last week and you can move at any time. You do not need to buy any furniture."

Ishtar looked at him "Thanks, You are an amazing man."

William looked at her and smiled while Ishtar held his hand happily then William said "I will give you the keys as soon as we reach the apartment."

"Sure." Ishtar said happily

As soon as they arrived Ishtar got into the kitchen while William held two empty glasses

"What are you doing?" William asked while he was looking at her

"I am trying to cook for you." Ishtar replied while she was standing infront of fridge

"I already ordered food." William said while Ishtar closed the fridge door and said "I want to cook today because it is your birthday."

"It is fine, do not worry."

Ishtar walked toward him "Can we see the apartment now, please?"

"Okay." William said then he set the glasses on a table. They got out of the kitchen and walked slowly to apartment'd door.

"Can I say something?" Ishtar said

William looked at her "Yes."

"I lost your apartment's key." Ishtar said slowly while William looked at her "Can I get another one?" she asked

William got the keys and said before he gave it to her "The gold one is for my apartment while the silver is for yours."

"Okay." Ishtar said happily while she was taking the keys from him

"You can lock the door." William said after they got out of the apartment

"Which floor is the apartment?" Ishtar asked when they were walking to the elevator

"The next floor." William said when they got into the elevator

Ishtar got out of the elevator before William and asked "which one?"

"Number 25." William said while Ishtar kept walking ahead of him. As soon as she found the apartment, she ran toward it. She opened the door happily and got into the apartment.

She started discorving the apartment while William got into the apartment and closed the door. He walked slowly behind her and asked "How is it?"

"It is amazing." She said then she sat on a chair

"Can you move so quickly to the apartment, please?"

Ishtar stood up and cuddled him "Sure, I will and thanks for everything."

William smiled then he kissed her while Ishtar looked at him and said "Next month I will be living here."

William's face shone "I am so happy to hear that."

Ishtar walked to the two bedrooms which they were beside each other and got into one of them. She looked through the window then opened the closet door then got out of it and entered the other one

"What do you think?" William asked while he was standing beside the door room

"My mother can get the biggest one." Ishtar said while she was closing the closet door then she walked toward William

"Shall we leave?" he asked

"Yes, let's celebrate your birthday." Ishtar said while William held her hand and got out of the apartment

"Next month this will be your apartment." William said to Ishtar when she was locking the apartment's door

Ishtar looked at him and smiled "I can not wait to move here." Then they got into the elevator. William held her face and kissed her "I can not wait to see you in a dancer costume."

Ishtar looked at him and smiled "I hope you will like it." They got out the elevator and walked toward William's apartment

William said when Ishtar was opening his apartment door "I bought you a costume also."

Ishtar looked at him confused then she said while she was putting the keys in her purse "why?"

"I like it."

"Which colour?" Ishtar asked while they were walking together to the kitcken

"Red." William said while he was holding a bottle of wine

Ishtar smiled and held two empty glasses then they walked together to William's bedroom. William set the bottle on a night table and looked happily at Ishtar, who already got into the bed. At that moment the door bell rang "The food is here." William said then he added while he was getting out of the room "Prepare yourself while I am preparing the food."

Ishtar got out of the bed and opened the bottle of wine. She was pouring for herself when William came back with a tray of food and shots of vodka

"I brought vodka shots." William said while he was setting the tray on the night table then he looked at Ishtar passionately and held her hand and pulled her toward him then he took her glass of wine and set it beside the food. His left hand got down to her waist while his right hand held her chin. Then he unzipped her dress by his left hand and took it off. He started rubbing her neck by his right hand then he moved his index finger to the space between her breasts while his left hand unhooked her bra then he took it off.

They gazed at each other for seconds then Ishtar took off his shirt then she unbuttoned William's pants. She got into the bed and pulled him toward her. She layed down on her back and opened her legs while William leaned over her. He started kissing her lips then got down to her breast and stomach. Finally he took off her panties while Ishtar looked passionately at him. After more than a half an hour William and Ishtar was relaxing naked on the bad. Then Ishtar moved toward William and rested her head on his chest while William got glass of wine and gave it to her

"I am so hungry." She said while she was adjusting her position and getting her glass of wine. William got off the bed and wore his clothes then he moved to his closet and got off the belly dancer custom

"Do you want to wear it?" William said while he was looking at Ishtar, who sipped from her drink then got off the bed and walked naked toward him. The costume contains from bra and skirt in red colour. The bra has red beads hanging down. The bottom was red chiffon skirt which has two thigh high slit. There was also a red belly dancing isis wings for wearing around the neck.

Ishtar said "You bought the same as the dancer was wearing."

"Yes, I did." William said then he asked "Is it same as yours?"

"No."

"Can you wear this one, please?"

"Sure." Ishtar held the costume

"You have to dance for me."

"I am not a good dancer."

"I do not care."

"Okay, it is your birthday so you can have what ever you want." Ishtar said then she gave the glass of wine to William and started wearing the costume while William tried to help her. As soon as she finished wearing, she looked at the mirror. She adjusted her bra and the skirt then she looked happily at William.

"You look stunning." William said while Ishtar covered William's face by her isis wings. William smiled then he got into the bed "You can dance now."

Ishtar smiled then she walked toward him. She shook her shoulders then covered William's face again by her Isis wings then pulled them slowly and turned around herself while her hands were open widely. William was looking at her happily then he got vodka shot while Ishtar kept dancing. He seemed happy and excited while Ishtar started shaking her hip first the right hip then the left hip while her hands were up then she shook her hips both at one time then shook her shoulders while William was looking at every part of her body. She covered again his face by her isis wings, but at this time William held them. He stood up and moved slowly toward her while he was still holding her isis wings while Ishtar looked happily at him. She put her hands on his shoulder and smiled while William surrounded her waist by his arms then he kissed her.

"I love you." He said

Ishtar looked happily at him and said "You are the most beautiful thing happened to me."

William kissed her forehead then he asked "Why do not you sleep here?"

"I will but first I have to go home and see my mother and after she will fall asleep, I will return here."

"Okay, I agree." William said then he held her hand and sat together on a bed. He gave Ishtar her glass of wine and he got his glass while he set the food infront of them

"My sister and her husband are going to their honey moon in beginning of the next month."

William looked surprise "I thought they do not want to have honey moon."

"Yea right, but now they want to leave the city."

William thought for seconds then he asked "Where do you want ours to be?"

Ishtar looked at him "Paris or rome."

"Big or small wedding."

"Small wedding."

William looked at her "Any specific time."

"Yes, fall. And I want it in a park."

William looked at her "Why?"

"Fall is my favourite season."

"Okay this is just an option."

"Okay." Ishtar said then she touched her bra "I am going to take off this costume."

"Why?"

"They are not comfortable." Ishtar said then she got off the bed. She took the costume off; she wore her clothes and returned back to her spot

"You do not want to bring some of your clothes here." William said

"If I moved next week to the new apartment, I would not bring any clothes to your apartment."

"Okay." William said then he looked at her and asked "Do you want a vodka shot?"

"Yes, I do."

William got out the bed and looked at Ishtar while he was saying "I will come back."

Ishtar set her empty glass of wine on the night table then she took the belly dance custom and hanged in the closet then she walked to the kitchen but she was surprised when she did not find William there. She got out and looked for him finally she heard a voice coming from a balcony. She smiled then she got out and walked toward William, whom was talking on his phone. Ishtra inhaled then she looked down at the crowded streets

"It was Patrick." William said as soon as he finished his phone call

"Is he okay?"

"Yes, he called to say happy birthday and to remind me about the meeting tomorrow."

"Which meeting?" Ishtar asked

"With one of his colleague."

Ishtar looked at him and said sadly "Can I come back after I leave?"

"Yes, you can come any time you want."

"I thought you have to leave early tomorrow."

"We can leave together." Ishtar smiled while William held her face in her both hands and looked at her shinning eyes

"You are every thing for me. I wish everyday wake up while you are next to me. My days are so bored and long without you."

Ishtar looked at him and said "You are my everthing."

They kissed and embraced each other then he held her hand and walked to the room together. They got into the bed together then William said "I forgot to bring shots."

"We can drink later when I come back here." Ishtar said while she was holding his left hand to prevent him from leaving the room

William looked at her and said "Okay."

"I will take a taxi for work tomorrow." Ishtar said while she was pouring wine in her glass

"You need a car."

Ishtar looked at him and said "I do not like driving and next week I be living in your building."

William smiled "You can call my driver anytime you want." Then William said while he was touching Ishtar's hair "You have very long hair.You need a hair cut."

Ishtar touched her hair then she started to braid it "I will book an appointment for next week after I will move here."

William looked at her "Are you going to change your hair style?"

Ishtar looked at him "Why?"

William sighed then he said after seconds of thought "I do not know. I just do not like your hairstyle."

"What?"

"It is so long."

Ishtar seemed disappointed "I like it."

"You can try different style."

Ishtar looked at her hair then she asked "I still do not know why my hair is bothering you."

"We share same bed and sometime the length bothers me." William said while Ishtar said nothing.

After few minutes Ishtar looked at William, who was eating and changing the television channel. She set her glass of wine on the night table and looked at William "Are you going to leave the televation in the room?"

"Yes, why?"

"Televation ruins relationships."

"What?" William was surprise

Ishtar thought for seconds then she said "This is what I think."

William looked at her "No it does not." Then he stood up and took the food tray with him and left the room then he came back after few minutes he looked at Ishtar and said while he was sitting on bed heside her "You seemed disctrated. You do not have to cut your hair if you do not want."

Ishtar looked at him "I thought you do not like it."

"I do not like the length." William kept looking at Ishtar then he looked at her hair and pulled it

"What are you doing?" Ishtar yelled on him

William looked at her "You can keep your hair. I like this braid."

Ishtar looked at him and said sharpily "It is my hair." Then she took the bottle of wine to pour some drink for her "it is empty." She said

"What?" William was surprise then he added "i only drank one glass."

"Okay, okay." Ishtar looked at him "i drank the whole bottle."

"How?"

"I do not know." Ishtar said while William was smiling "Why are you smiling?" she asked him

"When i met you you were not drinking, today you mostly finish the whole bottle of wine." William said

"I shared the bottle with you."

"I drank vodka shot and my full glass of wine still there." William said while he was pointing on his glass of wine on the night table beside him

Ishtar looked upset at him then stood up "I think I have to leave now."

"Okay, let me tell my driver first." William said while he was standing then he held Ishtar's face and kissed her "Thanks for making my birthday perfect."

Ishtar looked happily at him while William's hand got down to her waist then he picked her up while Ishtar smiled and held his shoulders tightly then she kissed him.

William layed her down on the bed and leaned over her "You will come back here, right?" William said while he was rubbing her striped legs

"Yes, sure." she said happily

"The driver will take you back."

Ishtar sat on a bed and looked at William "You are coming with him, right!"

William looked at her "Yes."

"Okay, leave now." Ishtar said then they walked together and got out of room

Chapter Nine

THE LAST DAYS

"So you have no idea when Nazik is coming back from her honeymoon." Maria, who was breastfeeding her child, asked Ishtar when they were in Ishtar's new apartment while Ishtar was orgnazing her clothes in the closet

"No, she is not talking to me anymore."

"Why?"

Ishtar looked at her "Well, I asked her to move to the old building to help me with my mother and when she agreed I moved to new building."

"But she did not move. She still lives in her apartment."

"This is what I told her but she got angry and said that William is just controlling me."

Maria looked at Ishtar confused "Why? What did he do?"

"He bought me the apartment."

"Did he ask you before he bought the apartment?"

"No he bought it by himself."

Maria said after second of thought "Is the apartment under your name?"

Ishtar looked at her "What do you mean?"

Maria put her child in her stroller and walked toward Ishtar "Did you sign any papers?"

"No."

Maria sighed "did you meet a lawyer?"

"No."

"Did William give you the contart or any papers?"

"No." Ishtar stopped hanging the clothes and looked at Maria "Am I missing something?"

Maria took deep breath "I respect William but what he did is very wrong."

"You are frightening me." Ishtar sighed while Maria sighed "Can you explain please?" Ishtar asked

"He bought the apartment by himself, you did not see a lawyer or signatured any papers." Ishtar was listening carefully while Maria added "Maybe I am wrong but William is trying to control you."

"You are talking like my sister."

"Maybe we are wrong."

"How is he controlling me?" Ishtar asked after seconds of thought

"This is his apartment." Maria said

"He bought it for me."

"Why?"

"He is my fiancé and loves me."

"I know he is your fiancé and he loves you but people change."

"What do you mean?"

"Ask him about the purchase contarct." Maria said firmly while Ishtar looked at her and did not reply then Maria added "He is a good man I know but one day if you will have disagreement with him you have no place to go."

"I will be in my room."

"It will be his room also."

"What do I have to do?" Ishtar said sadly

"Your mother will live in this apartment as a result the apartment has to be under your name." Ishtar seemed disappointed while Maria added "Just talk to him."

"I do not want to argue with him."

"You have to discuss the subject with him." Maria said while Ishtar did not respond "I am hungry can we eat please."

"Yea, sure." They walked silently until they left the building then Maria said "You just have to ask him."

"Yes, I will."

Maria walked happily while she was pushing her daguther's stroller "You do not have to bring everything you have in your old apartment to the new apartment."

"I am not. I already have two bags of garbage."

"Wow already."

"Yea, some of them are my mother's clothes."

They entered a restaurant then they sat in patio. Maria inhaled "I like this area. I think I will move here."

"Yes, good so when William kick me out of the apartment, I can come over."

"Can you stop thinking about that?"

"Well, you told me about William's thoughts."

"Maybe I am wrong." Ishtar did not respond while Maria added "I just told you that so you can prepare for everthing."

"What do you mean?"

"As I told you people change, at beginning when i met you, you said that you want to keep your virginity until your wedding day but then you changed your thought and you lost your virginity while you are still unmarried."

"Well I am engaged."

Maria looked at her and said "You also were not drinking and now you do. Try not to be very optimistic."

Ishtar said madly "Okay, I will ask him about the apartment."

"You have to." Maria said while Ishtar did not respond then Maria asked "Are you going to stay working in iceream shop?"

"No, this Saturday is my last day."

"But you will stay working in library."

"Why will l quit my job in the library?"

"You keep changing your plans."

"No, I will stay there I need money." Then Ishtar said after second of thought "I am thinking of studying."

"Really!" Maria seemed excited

"Yes."

"What are planning to study?" Maria asked

"Maybe engineering." Ishtar said while Maria looked at her surprise then she said happily "You can study what ever you want. You are smart girl."

Ishtar smiled then she looked at Maria's daughter and said "Ana is awake."

"What?" Maria said then she whispered "she just slept ten minutes ago."

"She is quite."

"I have to change her diaper."

"We will leave after finish eating." Ishtar said then she looked at Ana "I can hold her if you want."

"If she cries, you are going to carry her."

Ishtar looked again at Maria's daughter and smiled "I still remember the day that she born. It was the first time I saw newborn baby."

Maria smiled "On that day I ruined your dress. I believe William was so disappointed and angry."

"Well, he bought something similar to the dress." Ishtar said

"Did he buy you a dress?"

"No, a costume." Ishtar said while Maria looked surprise "Is there something wrong if William bought me clothes?"

"No, some men buy clothes for their women."

"What about visiting family and freinds?"

"Are they annoying?"

"No, they are lovely."

"I used to make excuse when one of my boyfriends asked me to visit his family."

Ishtar smiled "You did not like his family, did you?"

"I did not like his mother."

"What did you do in the end?"

"I left him." Maria said then she smiled

"William asked me to join him, his best friend and his wife to watch some tennis matches with them during US open tennis."

"This is exciting." Maria seemed happy

"You think I should go."

"Yes, they are very enjoyable."

Ishtar sighed then she said "You think I should prepare myself."

"Yes, it is something you never regret." Maria said then she looked at her daughter, who was sleeping, and said "Can we leave? I want to check the area?"

"You still want to move."

"Yes, I will move and live beside my best friend."

"You do not have to."

"I want to." Maria said while Ishtar asked the waiters for the bill

"Do you have any thought about your wedding?" Maria asked Ishtar as soon as they got out of the restaurant

"Yes, we did talk about it."

"Which kind of wedding did you decide to have?"

"A small one."

"How many people?"

"Maybe 25 and in the park."

"Okay, I believe it will be perfect wedding." Maria said then she added when they walked through a park "You can do it in this park."

Ishtar looked at the park then she stopped. She looked happily at the big trees and green leaves and said happily "Actually it is good idea." then she looked at Maria "I will discuss this option with William."

"You can show him the park."

"Yes, sure." Ishtar said then she looked smiling at Maria and continued walking to the car so they can go back to their places

———✦———

"I thought your fiancée is coming with you." Patrick said to William when he opened the front door for him

"No, she wants to move to her new apartment so she is orgnazing her clothes."

"Will she move to live with you?" Patrick asked William when they were getting into the basement

"She is not moving to live with me."

"Why?" Patrick asked while he was getting beer from the fridge

"She can not leave her mother alone."

Patrick passed a can of beer for William and got one for himself then he said while he was sitting beside William "What about after you marry her?"

"She will divide her time between me and her mother."

"Oh, I think it is good idea."

"Why?" William asked after drinking from his beer

"You will have less drama and less arguement."

"Why will I have argument?"

"Becuase it happens."

"I believe we will be good after argue."

"Any way she will be living in your building thus you can see her anytime you want." Patrick said then he drank from his beer

"Maybe you are right." William said then he drank from his beer while Patrick turned on the television on "When will your kids come back home?" William asked Patrick

"I think they will come soon. They have been outside for awhile." Patrick said

"I miss them." William said then he added "Last time I saw them was in your son's baptism."

"My daughter is invited to her friend's birthday. They will watch movie first then eat in a restaurant in the end they will end up playing games in her freind's house." Patrick explained then he stood up he took the empty can of beers and went to the fridge to bring more can of beers then he asked when he was handling a can of beer to William "Who do you think will win the US open for this year?"

"I think Andy Roddick or Andre Agassi."

"You always cheer for them." Patrick said while he was sitting

"They are good." William said while he was opening his can of beer

"Yes, they are. I think Pete Sampras will win."

"Maybe, we will see."

"What about women?"

"Of course Venus Williams will get the champion." William said happily then he drank from his beer

Patrick nodded his head for agreement then he said "She will beat every one."

"We will go together to watch some matches, right?"

"Yes, sure."

"Ishtar already agreed to come with me also."

Patrick smiled "I guess she will cheer up your favourite players."

"Yea, she will." William said then he drank from his beer "Is Olivia still getting jealous from her brother?"

"Not like the beginning." Partick drank from his beer then he asked "Do you have any new plans for your wedding?"

"Yes, we planned." William said

"What did you plan?" Patrick asked happily

"She want small wedding and she has to marry in a church but no spicific day picked yet."

"She needs more time to prepare, right?" Patrick said

"Yes."

"Can Lisa help her?"

"Yes, she can. She can visit her anytime."

"What about you? When do you want to get married?"

"I want to get married as soon as possible but Ishtar does not want."

Patrick looked at him and smiled "Do you want to have family?"

"Of course I want to have family. I hove her to death so I want to have kids with her."

"I will ask Lisa to change Ishtar's thought about the wedding date."

"I hope she agrees to marry me as soon as possible."

"Did she mention any specific reason that prevents her from marrying you the time you want?"

William thought for seconds then he said "No."

"I think she is only nervous and anxious." William looked at him "You can ask her after sex." William looked puzzled while Patrick added "Yea, after sex she will be calm and relax."

William smiled "Okay, I can try that." William drank from his beer then he asked "What do I have to do if she does not change her mind?"

"Ask her again after long period of time from the first conversation."

"Few days."

"No, after two weeks."

"This is long."

"You have to be patient with her."

William seemed unhappy then he asked after seconds of silents "How is the management?"

"I am moving next week to a new office." Patrick said happily

"But you still in same floor, right?"

"Yes, I am."

William smiled "Okay I will see again in your new office or at some tennis matches." William stood up

"Are you leaving?" Patrick asked while he was standing up

"Yea, I am."

"But you did not see the kids."

"I will visit you soon. I have to drop Ishtar at her old apartment."

"Oh, she did not move yet."

"No, she said next month she will be ready to move."

"Your driver is waiting you, right?" Patrick asked William when they started walking together

"Yea, he is outside." They climbed the stairs together. Before William left Patrick's house he looked at him and said "We are going to watch some matches together, right?"

"Yea, sure." William said then he got out of front door

"Say, hi to Ishtar."

William looked at him and said "I will." Then he walked to his car and asked the driver to drive to his building.

As soon as he got into the building, he went to Ishtar's apartment. He looked for keys but he could not find them. He sighed then he rang the doorbell.

Ishtar was surprise when she opened the door "Oh, it is you."

William looked surprised then he got into the apartment and said while he was closing the door "Are you waiting someone."

"No." Ishtar said then they walked together

"So why you gave me the surprise look."

"You rang the bell instead of using your key." she said

"I could not find it." William said while Ishtar said nothing then William asked when he saw plates of rice, chicken breast and salad on a table"Are you eating?"

"Yes, I cooked and now it is time for me to eat and relax." Ishtar said while she was sitting on a table to eat

"I am hungry." William said while he was standing beside her

Ishtar looked at him "There is more food in the kitchen. You can have from there." Ishtar started eating while William went to the kitchen

"I thought you want to leave." William said when he came back and holding two plates in his hands

"I will leave later. I was so hungry."

"Why do not you sleep with me tonight?" William asked while he was sitting beside her

Ishtar looked at him "Maybe, I will."

William looked at her happily "We can sleep her in your apartment if you want."

"She is your apartment. You bought it."

"I bought it for you." William seemed excited while Ishtar seemed disappointed and distracted. She was remembering Maria's conversation about William buying her an apartment "Your food is delicious." William said while Ishtar did not respond

"Are you alright?" he asked

"Yes, I am."

"I was talking about your food."

"Do you like it?"

"Yes, I do." William said happily then he added "Patrick said hi to you."

"Oh, how is he?"

"He is alright." William said then took some salad from the bowl and added to his chicken plate "His wife offers to help you if you need help for preparing to our wedding."

Ishtar looked at him "help for what?"

"For our wedding."

"We are not getting married soon, right?"

William looked at her and sighed "No, we are not."

"I guess I do not need help." Ishtar said while William looked at her and said nothing. They kept eating their food silently. After minutes William suddenly asked "Why do not we get married any time soon?"

"Why do we have to get married?"

"Why not?"

"How many times will we have the same conversation?" Ishtar was yelling

William rubbed her back by his right hand "Why do you lose your temper everytime we discuss about our marriage?"

"Because you are pressuring me."

William looked at her "I do not want to lose you again."

"You will never lose me." Ishtar said lovely "I love you and always will be with you."

"What are the reasons that make you reject an early wedding?" William said sadly

"There are dozens of reasons."

"Can you list them for me, please?" William seemed hopeless while Ishtar looked at him and said "I do not know."

"Are you afraid?"

Ishtar looked at him "Maybe."

William sighed then he kissed her forehead "I want to have family and share every sunrise and sunset with you."

Ishtar looked happily at him then she kissed him and later she started eating again while William looked at her and started rubbing her left leg while Ishtar looked happily at him then she asked "When was the last time you shave?"

"Few days ago."

"You should have beard." Ishtar said while she was touching his face by her right hand

"Why?" William was surprise then he withdrew his hand from Ishtar's leg and held her right hand and kissed it

"I just never saw you in beard or mustache."

"I shave everyday."

"Yes, it is always so smooth." Ishtar said while she was looking happily at him while William released her hand and said "So you like to see me in beard."

"Yes."

"Maybe I will stop shaving for a while." William said then he added "In the end of next month I am going to a business trip for days."

Ishtar was surprise "What?"

"I have to travel." William said then he added "Why do not you come with me?"

"No, I can not."

"Why?"

Ishtar looked at him "I can not leave my mother alone."

"You sister can stay with her."

"I do not ....."

Before she completed her sentence William said madly "Why do not you make any sacrifices for me?" he stood up then he looked at her and said "Even in the future when I have to travel, you can not be with me because of your mother."

"Well, I work also."

"Why do not you quit your job?"

"Why do I have to quit?"

"So you can come with me."

"I work so I can pay my bills?"

"I can give you money."

Suddenly Ishtar remembred what Maria told her about the connection about buying the apartment and controlling her so she said immediately "I do not want your money."

"Why?"

"I do not want to stay home and I need money."

"I told you I can give you money."

Ishtar stood up "Why everything it has to be about you? Why do you have to control every step in my life?"

"What?" William was surprise

"Yes, always." She moved closed to him "You want the wedding day to be the day you want and now you ask me to quit my job." Ishtar was counting on her fingers and yelling then she added "And before you bought me this apartment."

William opened his mouth in disbelief "I just said I want to marry you because I do not want to lose you. About quiting your job and buying the apartment it is because I need you always beside me so we can spend time together." William was calm and disappointed

"You just want to control me." Ishtar was yelling

"What are you talking about?" William was angry

"Yea, I am right. Even Maria told me that."

"What did she told you?" William yelled

"She said you want to control me."

William held her face his hand and said kindly "I am taking care of you. I am not controlling you. I love you and I always want to be with you."

He kissed her while Ishtar kissed him back. He looked at her and carried her to the couch. He layed her down and leaned over her. He pulled her dress and started rubbing her legs while he was kissing her. He took off her panties while Ishtar took off his belt and then unbutton his jeans. William opened widly her legs while Ishtar exposed her breast. In the end he made love to her.

"Why is Maria against me now?" William said while they were lying on the floor stripped from thier clother

Ishtar looked at him "No, she is not."

"Yes, she is. In the begining she told you to remove the television from bedroom and now she convinced you I am trying to control you when I bought you an apartment."

Ishtar grabbed her dress then she said while she was wearing it "She talked about the television to my sister and it was before her wedding." She stood up and looked at William and added "She told me about the apartment because of my mother condition."

William stood up "What about your mother?" he grabbed his clothes and started wearing them

"In future after we get married, she must have a place to live."

"The apartment is for you and hers." William said while he was standing beside Ishtar both dressed then he added "The apartment is under your name and we can see a lawyer any time you want to make everything legal."

Ishtar held his hands "Thank you."

"Can you talk to Lisa in your spare time please?"

"Yea, sure." Ishtar said then they sat on a couch again

"I am still hungry." William said

"I can cook something else."

"No, thanks." William said then they carried their empty dishes and walked together to the kitchen

"Why dose Lisa want to see me?" Ishtar asked while she was setting the dishes in the sink

William looked at her while he was holding an empty plate "She wants to talk to you about our marriage."

"Oh." Ishtar seemed surprise

William fulled his plates of chicken breast then he looked at Ishtar "She knows some designers and wants you to see their works."

Ishtar seemed cofused "But we did not set a date yet."

"We can pick a date now." William said while they were leaving the kitchen

"What?" Ishtar was shocked

"It is only a day with some strangers. You will only signature papers and see few new faces, please say yes." They both sat on a couch then William looked at her waiting for her respond while Ishtar looked at him and saw the hope and sadness in hs eyes. She loves this man and he loves her "Okay, let set date." Finally she said

William said happily "you want a small wedding in a park, right?"

"Right."

"Can we marry in fall or Christmas?"

"What?" Ishtar was surprise

"Please, choose." William said sadly

Ishtar took a deep breath "I can not marry in a park if it is Christmas."

"Fall."

"Next fall, agree."

"No, fall of this year." Ishtar did not respond "When will you be ready?"

Ishtar closed her eyes and sighed while William looked at her and said "This is the last time I will mention the marriage."

"Okay, we will marry in fall." Ishtar suddenly said while William looked in disbelief at her then he kissed her left hand "You are the most amazing woman I met."

Ishtar smiled "But I will still be living in this apartment with my mother."

William looked at her "Agree." Then turned the televation on

"Did you watch any tennis matches?" Ishtar asked

"No, I did not." William said then he looked at her and added "If you want to come with me, we can go and watch any match."

"Maybe."

William changed a televation channel "Are you going to sleep here?"

"I do not know."

"Tomorrow is Saturday."

Ishtar stood up "I am going to call my sister."

William looked at her and did not respond then he started eating his chicken breast. After few minutes, Ishtar came back. She looked happily at him and announced "I can stay and sleep here."

William looked happily at her then he asked "Can we sleep in my apartment, please?"

"Yes, sure." Ishtar said while she was sitting then she looked at him and asked "Can we sleep in the cottage, please?"

"Yea, sure, then we can see my mother tomorrow."

"Yea, sure."

"Good, I am going to tell her when we reach the cottage." William said while he was standing then he held his empty plate and went to the kitchen then Ishtar followed him. They cleaned up the dishes then they got out of the kitchen. They walked together and got out of the building then they got into the car

"My mother will be so happy when she heard the news." William said to Ishtar when they were sitting in the back of the car

"I know. It has been so long since I saw her."

"She always asks me about you."

"We can visit her from time to time, if you want."

"Of course I want but I thought you do not like the idea."

"No, it is fine with me."

William looked at her and said happily "Good."

After more than half an hour they reach the cottage. It was sunset time. The driver drop them then he left while William and Ishtar walked to the cottage. Before they got into the cottage, William decided to call his mother and let her know that he is visiting her with Ishtar tomorrow. Ishtar looked at him and walked far from him toward the water.

As soon as William finished his call, he looked for Ishtar then he walked toward her happily after he found her. Ishtar looked smiling at him when William stood beside her. He sat beside her on the sand and looked at the sunset. Ishtar leaned on him and kept looking at the sunset

"Do you like sunset?" he asked while he was putting his left arm on her

"Yes."

After few seconds William asked "What are you thinking?"

Ishtar said without looking at him "Nothing."

"Is it thinking about marriage stressing you?"

Ishtar hesitated before she said "Maybe."

William started rubbing her back by his left hand then he rubbed her left shoulder while he was saying "Everything will be alright."

Ishtar looked at him and said happily "I know."

After few seconds William said "I am trying to remember the wedding dress that you tried with your sister."

Ishtar looked at him "Oh yea. If you want, we can go together there so I can try some of the dresses."

"Yea, sure." William said while Ishtar looked at the sunset and then she looked back at William, who was looking at her and smiling then they kissed

"You are the most amazaing thing happened to me." Ishtar said while William kissed her again "Tomorrow after leaving your mother house, I can try some dresses." Ishtar said while William nodded his head happily

After the senset William stood up and helped Ishtar to stand up then they walked back to the cottage

"Can I say something?" Ishtar asked

"Yes ofcourse."

"When you asked me about choosing the time to get married, I was so anxious." Ishtar looked at him "But now I just want to be with you."

William stopped and looked at her then he held her face in his hands and said warmly "I love you."

"I love you too." Ishtar said then they kissed each other. Then William held her hand and continued walking toward the cottage. Before they got into the cottage William asked "Can we get married here?"

"Where?"

"In front of the cottage." William opened the door then he pointed on a beach "The ceremony will be on the beach."

"My sister got married on a beach."

"You can marry on the beach too."

"No, I do not want."

William sighed "Can you at least think about it, please?"

"Yea, sure." Ishtar said while she was getting into the cottage then she added "Last time I was here, it was when I got engaged." William locked the door and looked at her smiling while Ishtar said "I have unforgettable memories here." Ishtar looked at William "We should come here more often."

"Any time you want we can come here."

Ishtar walked few steps forward "Maybe, I will marry here."

"You change your mind."

"I said maybe." Ishtar said with a smile

"Okay, it is time to have drink." William said happily then he held her hand and walked to the kitchen. He opened the fridge and got two cans of beer then they walked into the room. He opened one can of beer and passed to Ishtar, who was sitting on a bed then he opened the other can of beer and drank from it while he was sitting beside Ishtar on the bed. William turned the television on while Ishtar asked "What time will we go to your mother's house tomorrow?"

"In the afternoon." William said

"So we are going to eat there."

"Yes." William said then he drank from his beer then he said while he was looking at the room "When you broke up with me, I came here." Ishtar looked at him while William added without looking at her "I was so devastated and angry. I called Patrick and he came immediately here." Ishtar seemed sad while William continued "He stayed here the whole night. We drank and played video game. In the morning when I woke up, I was sleeping on a couch covered by blanket while he was sleeping on a chair."

Ishtar set her can of beer on a night table beside her and approached William "I am sorry for the pain I cost."

William smiled "That was in the past. Now we are engaged."

Ishtar smiled "I did not know you play video games."

"Only when I am angry and so bored." William said then he stood up and went to the kitchen and brought more beer while Ishtar layed down on the bed

"Are you tired?" William asked while he was gettint into the bed

"Yes."

"We can sleep any time you want." William said while Ishtar yawned and said nothing. After less than an hour they slept peacefully

In the next morning Ishtar woke up before William. She went to the kitchen to find something to prepare for breakfast but she did not find bread or eggs in a fridge. She sighed and went back to the room. She got a towel and a robe and went to the bathroom to take a shower. After few minutes inside the shower, a shower curtain opened and William jumped into the bath tub. Ishtar looked at him and said "You are not allowed here."

"Some water, please." William said while Ishtar turned her back to him and turned on the faucet "You woke up early." William said while they were waiting for the water to warm enough. Ishtar looked at him "Yes, I did." Then she passed him the shower gel after she used it "You have nothing in your fridge to eat or cook."

William looked at her "We can eat breakfast after leaving." Then he held the handheld shower in his left hand and started rinsing Ishtar's body. He was rubbing her body in his right hand and carrying the shower head holder in his left hand while Ishtra was looking passionately at him. After they washed their body William dried Ishtar's body then he dried his. He carried Ishtar to the bed room and made love to her.

After they ate thier breakfast, they bought some frozen items and breakfast food and went back to the cottage.

"I bought them because you insisted." William, who was carrying the bags, said while Ishtar was opening the door

"We need them." Ishtar said while William got into the cottage "next month we will come back here. I love this place." She added then they walked to the kitchen. William set the bags on a table. He opened the bags started handling the iteams to Ishtar who was organizing the items inside the fridge.

"Any time you want we can come and sleep here."

"I have very special memories here." Ishtar said happily

"You can have the key's door. I already have another one." William said then he held Ishtar's hand and walked to the living room and sat on a couch

"We will increase our time here, right?" Ishtar said while she was touching William hair

"Yes, we will." William said kindly

"Even in winter we can come here and sit infront of the fireplace while we are drinking." Ishtar said

William looked at her "And I can take your clothes off." Ishtar smiled and leaned on his right shoulder while William embraced her with his both hands "Mostly my mother and her husband spend time here."

Ishtar looked at him "So we have to share the cottage with them."

"No, my time with you is very privet." William said then he kissed her head and added "We can just arrange the time same as we do with your sister when you ask her to stay with your mother."

"Okay." Ishtar said then she rested her head on his chest and satyed silent while William turned the television on. After more than five minutes William asked Ishtar, who was silent "Are you alright?"

"Yes, I am."

"If you want, we can cancel going to my mother's house."

"No, I am just tired."

"I guess, you did not have enough sleep."

"Yea, I had a bad dream."

"What was about?"

"I was in the middle of cemetery alone."

"What?" William was shocked

"And I seemed lost."

"It is only a dream." William said then he kissed her left hand "You do not have to worry about it."

"But the cemetery was beside the beach." Ishtar said while William looked surprise at her

"Let's go to my moher's house." William said then he helped Ishtar to stand up.

As soon as they arrived his mother's house the dogs where barking on each other in William's mother garden

"Why are they barking on each other?" William asked his mother when they stood beside her

"I do not know." Margaret said then she looked happily at Ishtar and hugged her "I missed you." She said kindly

Ishtar smiled "I missed you too."

Margaret's mother held one the dogs and walked away from them while William held another dog but the dogs kept barking on each other

"Are you hungry?" Margaret said when they got into the house

"Yes, we are?" William said then he walked away from them while his mother and Ishtar went to the kitchen and sat around the table

"How are you?" William's mother asked Ishtar

"I am alright."

She got very close to Ishtar then she whispered "Can you increase your visit to here please? I am missing you."

Ishtar looked at her and said kindly "Yes, sure."

At that moment William got into the kitchen "Where did you leave the dog?" his mother asked him

"With Martin."

"Oh, I thought your brother is not here." William's mother said

"No, he is in his room." William said while he was sitting on a chair beside Ishtar

"Do the dogs always bark on each other?" Ishtar asked

"No, they are not." Margaret said then she looked at William and asked him "You should visit me often."

"I am always busy with her." William said while he was pointing on Ishtar, who looked surprise at him

"You can visit her with me or without me." Ishtar said

"I am always with you."

"You can come together." His mother said while she was looking at Ishtar

"Sometime I have to stay with my mother." Ishtar said

"How is your mom?"

"She is fine."

"Is she alone at home now?"

"No, she is with my sister."

"Oh, so your sister can always be with her when you are here."

"Yes, sometime she can sometimes she can not because she is married." Ishtar said while William's mother seemed disappointed

"Okay let's eat." Margaret said after seconds of silence then she stood up. William looked at his mother and stood up after her then Margaret looked happily at Ishtar and said "I can not wait to share thinkgiving with you."

"I am waiting for fall also." William said while he was following his mother

"Did you miss the turkey?" his mother, who was holding a plate of fried fish, asked

"No, I did not." William said while he was taking the plate from her

His mother looked surprise at him then she held a tray of chicken and asked him while she was getting back to the table "What did you miss in fall?"

"We are getting married in fall." William announced

"What?" his mother was shocked then she looked at Ishtar, whom said while she was standing "Yes, we are."

"When did you decide to get married in fall?" Margaret asked Ishtar

"Yesterday." Ishtar said with a smile

"Which kind of wedding will be?"

"Friends and family and in a park."

"I am so happy." Margaret said then she embraced them together "I can not wait for fall to come in." Margaret added happily then she went back to the oven and held a tray of cooked potatoes and asked while she was setting the tray on the table "Did you find a dress?"

"No, not yet. I am going with Lisa to see some wedding dresses." Ishtar said while William's mother embraced her again happily then she looked at William and said "I can not believe you are getting married." William smiled and said nothing while his mother said happily "This is the happiest thing I have ever heard in my entire life. We have to drink."

She walked far from them happily while William and Ishtar looked at her. She came back with a bottle of champagne while William stood up and grabbed empty glasses. She gave the bottle to William and said wormly "I have been waiting for this news for years."

William looked at her then he embraced her. After few seconds William's mother said while she was looking at Ishtar "Since the first time I saw you, I felt you are the one." Ishtar looked warmly at her and said nothing while William opened the bottle and poured drink for each one of them then all of them held their full glasses.

"To my amazing son and his true love." His mother said while William and Ishtar said together "To us." Then they drank from thier glasses

"I hope by getting married you will encourage your sister to get married." William's mother said when they started eating

"She thinks it is early for her." William said

"No, it is not. She has been engaged for long time." His mother said

"Well, I hope she will decide soon." William said then he added happily "Ishtar now lives in my building."

"Why do not you move to live with him?" William's mother asked Ishtar

"Maybe after marriage. I have to take care of my mother." Ishtar said

"I guess you need a house after marriage."

They looked at each other "I do not like housese." Ishtar said

"I think later you will change your mind."

"Maybe."

"I am going to buy a car for Martin?" William asked

"He does not need a car." William's mother said

"It is his birthday gift."

"You can purchase the car later."

"Okay I ask you before I buy it."

"This food is so delicious." Ishtar said

"My husband helped me in cooking." William's mother said

"Is he a chef?" Ishtar asked

"No, he only helps me when I need help." William's mother said then she asked William "Have you watched any tennis match?" his mother asked

"No, I did not. I am so busy with her and Patrick."

"Oh, I did not see him for months. I guess I will see him again at your wedding."

"Yes."

"Maria will be attended the wedding also." Ishtar said while William looked at her

"I know." Then he poured more drink for him and his mother "Maybe tomorrow we will see the lawyer."

"Okay." Ishtar said then she looked at him and asked "when do you want us to watch one of the tennis matches?"

William sighed "I have no idea but mostly the finale match we are going to watch." He looked at her and asked "I thought you are not fan of tennis."

"I am not a fan but I do not mind watching it with you." William smiled then he kissed her forehead. After few seconds of thought William's mother suggested while she was holding her glass of drink "If you want, you can marry in the backyard of the house."

William and Ishtar looked at each other "I like the idea." William said happily

"You can do what ever you want." William's mother said then she set her glass of drink on the table and added while she was moving her both hands "you can add or remove things, do whatever you want."

"Actually William suggested earlier to have a wedding on the beach of his cottage." Ishtar said

"What did you decide?" William's mother seemed curious and excited

"I do not know." Ishtar said

"You can do what ever you want?" William said with a smiled while Ishtar looked at William and his mother and said nothing.

"You can choose another place to celecrabte your wedding." William's mother said

Ishtar sighed then she said "I believe I will choose a wedding on the beach near the cottage over the house."

William smiled while his mother said "It is your wedding." Then she looked at Ishtar's glass which was emepty and asked "Do you want more drink?"

"Yes, please?" Ishtar said while she was extending her right arm

"Any other plans for your wedding?" William's mother said while she was pouring more drink for Ishtar

William looked at Ishtar, whom seemed confused, and said "We can plan later it is only small ceremony."

"Do you still have a best man?" Ishtar asked

"Yea, Patrick will be."

"You will keep the tradition even it is a small wedding, right?" William's mother said

"Yes, we can include his kids in the wedding if you want." William said to Ishtar

"He is your best friend and his daughter could be included." Ishtar said

"You can discuss the details with Lisa when you go with her to see some wedding dresses." William said

"I thought we are going together."

William looked at her "You can do both."

"Which kind of flowers are you going to choose?" William's mother asked while Ishtar looked at her and said "I do not know."

"I can help you if you want." William's mother said happily while Ishtar smiled and nodded her head for agreement.

After that William and Ishtar left the house and went to bridal shop to see some wedding dresses. After she tried two of them, they left the store and headed to Ishtar's old apartment to drop here there.

Chapter Ten

LIFE AFTER LOSING WILLIAM

On next month Ishtar saw a lawyer and signature the apartment's papers then she moved with her mother to the new apartment. She also shopped with Lisa for her wedding dress unfortunately she did not like any one of them so they planned to go again

"Do you want to come with us to shop for wedding dress?" Lisa asked William and her husband while they were sitting infront of William's cottage drinking beer after they watched the last match of US open tennis

"No, not today." William said while he was holding his bottle of beer

"Why do I have to be with you?" Patrick asked

"Becuase we are all together." Ishtar said

"You two can go anywhere but William and I will stay here." Patrick said

"Okay you can stay here and keep drinking." Lisa said

"Better than shopping." Patrick said happily

"I guess they are disappointed because of the match." Ishtar said to Lisa

"I know. They hoped Andy Roddick would win the champion." Lisa said while she was looking at William and Patrick then she added "But he did not."

"Yes, we are already in bad mood and we can not go anywhere." William said then he drank from his beer

"When are you going to travel?" Patrick asked

"Next week. I will see the lawyer first then I will come to see you and bring the papers."

"Which papers?" Ishtar asked

William looked at her then he said after seconds hesitation "They are just papers about the job."

"Are you traveling with him?" Lisa asked Ishtar

"No, she does not want." William said while he was looking at Ishtar

"I want but I can not." Ishtar said sharply

"Yea, I know because of you mother." William said

"Yea, because of my mother." Ishtar said

"We have to see wedding dresses." Lisa said

After seconds of thought Ishtar said "I am going to buy a wedding dress and you are not going to see it until wedding day."

William looked at her and said happily "Actually this is brilliant idea. I do not want to see the dress until the wedding day."

"Why do you want to see her in the wedding dress before the weddng day?" Patrick asked

"She insisted to see her wearing the wedding dress." William said

"I just want you to come with me for shopping." Ishtar said

"I hate shopping."

"I know but this time is so different."

"So you change your mind now."

"No, i did not. I will go with Lisa and purchase the dress while you are away."

"I agree."

"The first time I saw Lisa wearing the wedding dress was on our wedding day." Patrick said while he was looking at Ishtar

William looked at him and asked "His mother helped her, right?"

"Yes, she did."

"Next week we can see the dresses. I already contacted some designers." Lisa said

"Okay, sure." Ishtar said

"Can we get more beer please?" William asked Ishtar

"Why do not you get it by yourself?" Ishtar asked

"Because I am in bad mood."

Ishtar stood up and said "Because you are lazy."

"Please, some beer." William said while he was holding her right hand

"Sure." Ishtar said then she got into the cottage

"Is it Ishtar's idea or yours to get married here?" Patrick said while he was looking at the beach and holding his bottle of beer in his right hand

"Ishtar's idea." William said

"The wedding will be great here." Lisa said while Ishtar got out of the cottage with half dozen bottle of beer

"We can also see the decorative flowers next week when we look for a dress." Lisa said to Ishtar

"Yes, sure." Ishtar said

"Will we have a cake?" William asked

"Yes, ofcourse." Ishtar said

"I hope the cottage will help us during the wedding."

"Yea, it will."

"I want to say the vow during sunset then later we can celebrate." Ishtar said

"We can buy candles and surround the place." Lisa said

Ishtar looked happily at her "Yes, I want alot of candles and flowers."

"Okay we will buy them next week." Lisa said

"Sure and if you have more plan just tell me about it." Ishtar said while Lisa nodded her head happily. After more than an hour Patrick and Lisa left the cottage while William and Ishtar left the cottage after the sunset

On Tuesday, September, 11, 2001 William woke up early. He met the lawyer and then headed to Patrick's work at first World Trade Centres

"What is the most important thing that you want to discusses with me before your travel?" Patrick asked William when they sat on a couch in Patrick's office

"I just want you to save some papers her." William said while

"What papers?" Patrick, who was confused, asked

"I bought a house for Ishtar in Manhatton but she does not know as a result I want you to keep the papers here in your office." William said while he was showing Patrick the papers

"You bought a house."

"Yes."

"When are you planning to tell her?" Patrick asked while he was checking the papers

"After marriage."

"Is it going to be only for her or you can share it?"

"Actually it will be our future house."

Patrick looked happily at him and asked "How many kids are you planning to have?"

"Two, just like you."

"Maybe I will have more."

William smiled "Maybe I will change my mind about the number."

Patrick smiled then he stood up and opened a saver beside his desk and hid the papers there then he looked at William "They are in save place now."

"Do not let Lisa to know please? Defiantly she will tell Ishtar."

"No, I am not going to tell her." Patrick said when he was walking back to his spot "Why did not you hide the papers in your apartment?"

"I can not. Ishtar is always there. She will see it and I do not trust my mother because she will keep asking me to see the house." William said while Patrick sat beside him

"Do not worry, the papers are safe here."

William smiled "I know."

"When will you travel?"

"Next week on Wednesday." William responded

"I guess I will see you before you travel."

"Yes, sure. Ishtar already bought the candels and chose the flowers."

"This is good."

"Yes, and she has the guest list."

"How many?"

"Close to 35 guest."

"Good, you have plenty things are already done."

"Yea, thanks to Lisa."

Patrick smiled then he asked "What do you want to drink?"

"I can have coffee."

"Okay." Patrick said then he stood up and walked to his desk. He picked up the phone and asked for two coffees

"Do you have any meeting today?" William asked

"No, I do not." Patrick said while he was returning back to his seat

After few minutes their coffee arrived.

"Are you going to leave Ishtar to decide everything about the wedding?" Patrick asked

"Yea, she can do what ever she wants." William smiled "I just want to see her wearing the wedding dress and then get married."

Suddenly they heard a loud noise from outside then something fell down. Both looked at each other wondering about the noice

"What is happening?" William asked Patrick

"I do not know." Patrick said then he stood up

"I think it is a clinet fighting with workers." William said

"I do not think it is one person."

"The building is secured, right?"

"Yes."

Patrick said then he walked few steps forward from the door

"What is this smell?" William asked after he started sniffing a strange smell

After few seconds Patrick said "I smell smoke."

"I also smell it."

"I am going to see what is happening." Patrick said then he walked toward the door

"Wait." William said then he stood up while Patrick stopped and looked at William "I am coming with you." William said then he walked toward Patrick

As soon as Patrick opened the door, both stepped out of the room and looked around them. The smoke was covering all the rooms and it was increasing. People were running and others were using their phones. Patrick, who seemed panic, looked at William and asked "What is going on?"

"Ask someone." William, who was afraid, asked while Patrick moved quickly and stopped someone but he did not get the answer. Patrick stopped at his spot and started coughing then he looked at William and walked back to him

"Your phone is ringing." William said slowly while he was also coughing

Patrick got the phone out of his pocket "Hello."

"What is going on?" the voice asked

Patrick looked at William and said "It is Lisa." Then he sat on the floor. At that moment William remembered Ishtar and grabbed his phone from his pocket and dialed her number while he was coughing but there was no answer beacause Ishtar was organizing some of the returned books at the library

"Do you need help?" Ishtar co-worker asked when she stood beside her

"Yea, sure." Ishtar said with a smile then she added "I am hungry."

"You can take a break. I will do the rest." Her co-worker said while Ishtar smiled and walked far from her. As soon as she opened her locker, she got her phone and looked at it. She felt terrible when she saw William's name on the missing calls. She got into the washroom and called William "Are you alright?" she asked

"Yea," William hardly replied he coughed then he said "I do not think I will make it." William hardly said

"What?"

"If I have to choose the woman that I have to fall in love with her I will choose you again without any hesitation." William said slowly while Ishtar seemed confused and afraid "Is everything okay? I can not understand what you are saying. I only hear very loud noise." she asked while William added "Even though our relationship is very complicated, I do not regret any moment that I spent it with you."

"I can not understand what you are saying." Ishtar said while William sighed and looked at Patrick, who was lying on the floor and not moving. William closed his eyes and coughed hardly

"Hello, William!" Ishtar, who was disappointed, said while William dropped his phone and walked hardly toward Patrick and tried to wake him up but Patrick did not move then William looked around himself and saw a person jumped from the window in trying to survive from the flame. The smoke was covering the building and most of people were not moving. He coughed then he layed down beside Patrick. He closed his eyes and remembered Ishtar, who tried to call him but he did not answer her call then she looked disappointed at her cell phone and said "I wish I could hear the whole conversation." Then she got out of the washroom. She looked at her cell phone again then left it in her locker. She thought of William then she left the staff room and went back to her co- worker

"Oh, you came back early." Ishtar's co-worker said when Ishtar stood infront of her. Ishtar did not reply and seemed unhappy and distracted

"Are you okay?" her co-workers asked

"No, I am not." Ishtar said

Her co-worker looked at her "What happened?"

Ishtar took a deep breathe "I called my fiancé and when he replied I was not able to understand what he was saying."

"Call him again."

"I did but he did not respond."

"Maybe he is driving or he is working."

"I feel something bad happeed to him." Ishtar said sadly

"What?"

"He said I do not... I could make it."

Her co- worker looked at her and said "Call him again." But Ishtar did not respond

"He is just busy. Call him again in few minutes." Her co-worker said then she rubbed Ishtar's left arm "Have some rest." She said then they walked together to the rest room. Ishtar sat on a chair while he co- worker asked "Do you need water?"

Ishtar looked at her and said "No thanks I am better now."

As soon as her co-worker left Ishtar asked herself about what happened to William but she could not find any clue. She tried to call him again but again he did not reply. Definitely something happened to him and what he was trying to tell her when she called him. That loud noise bothered her.

Suddenly she asked herself "Did he travel early to his business trip and he was trying to tell me what he did while he was on the plane?" She shook her head in disbelieve then she stood up and sighed "I can not believe he was trying to say goodbye on the phone before he travelled." Ishtar looked at the door and felt anger and disappointed instead of afraid and panic. She walked into the fridge and drank water. "I am not going to call him again." She said herself in anger then she left the room and returned back to her co-worker.

"Are you alright?" her co- worker asked when she saw her

"Yes, I am." Ishtar replied

"Did you call your fiancé?"

"No, I just figure out what he wanted to say." Ishtar seemed careless while her co-worker said nothing. After few minutes their supervirour came on "Julia can you cover Taylor's section please?" she said to Ishtar co-workers

"Yea, sure, is she in her break?"

"No, she left."

"Left! Was she sick?"

"No, she left because of what is happening."

"What is happening?" Ishtar, who seemed panic, asked

"She has cousin works in one of tower thus she left."

"Which tower?" Ishtar seemed curious

"World Trade Centres."

"What happened to towers?" Ishtar was afraid

"I think she said there is an explosion in the tower."

"What?" Ishtar was shock

"This is what she told me."

"When did that happen?" Ishtar's co-worker asked

"Half an hour ago or less."

"But I did not here anything." Ishtar said

"The library is so far from the towers so we did not know about the explosion."

"An explosion! How did that happen?" Ishtar's co-worker asked

"I do not know."

"I think you are wrong." Ishtar, who was anxious, said

"I hope." The supervisor said then she walked far from them

Ishtar sighed and seemed disappointed while her co-worker asked "Do you know someone works there? A friend or relative?"

Ishtar took a deep breath "My fiancé's best friend works there and my fiancé is going to see him today."

"You can call your fiancé and ask him what happened." Ishtar's co-worker said while Ishtar did not reply

"If you need me I will be in history section." Ishtar's co-worker said before she left while Ishtar looked at her and said nothing. Ishtar walked quickly and went back to staff room. She got her phone and got out of the library. She sighed and called William but there was no respond. She hoped to hear his voice and tell her that they are out of the towers but that did not happen. She sighed and called again and again but there was no reply. She rubbed her forehead and looked anxiously on her phone waiting for William to call her. She closed her eyes and asked herself "What happened to him and his phone? What is happening with him?" she opened her eyes and thoughts started jumpeing to her head "Maybe his phone had been broken or maybe he is out to eat breakfast with Patrick."

Remembering William's best friend made her so desperate and anxious. She breathed a long sigh and said "I think he visited Patrick this morning." She looked around herself in hope to see William coming from somewhere to see her and tell her what he wanted to say when he called her but that did not happen. She looked at her phone and said "He is alright…. He is fine.…..He is working now.……He just travelled earlier than his travel plan." she kept convincing herself her fiance is alright and alive and rejected any negative thoughts about him. She looked at her engagement ring and held it tightly "He is safe and alive." she said herself then she kissed her engagement ring and walked fast to get into the library. She sat on a chair and lowered her head then she rested her head in her hands and closed her eyes. She looked at her phone but there was nothing. Again thoughts of William being with Patrick inside the tower started haunting her.

Where could he be? Why is not he answering his phone? What did happen to his phone? All of those thoughts were in Ishtar's mind. She kept distracted and could not find an answer for her questions. Suddenly an idea came to her mind. She immediately called Maria and asked her to come to the library and pick her from her work

"Are you okay?" Maria asked Ishtar when she got into the car

"No, I am not." Ishtar said

"What happened?"

"Can you drive to World Trade Centres?"

"Why?"

"Drive please." Ishtar was angry

After few minutes from driving Maria asked "Do you know the towers are not safe now?"

"I know."

"Can I know why we are going there please?"

"I think William is there."

"What?" Maria was shocked "Who told you?"

"He said he will see Patrick before he travels."

"Maybe he is not there."

"I do not know."

"Did you see him in the morning?"

"No, I left early morning. His driver dropped me at work."

"Maybe you are wrong."

Ishtar sighed "I hope."

"Why do not you call him?"

"I did but there is no answer." Ishtar closed her eyes and said sadly and hardly "He called me earlier but I was not able to understand everything he said."

"Why?"

"I do not know. It was too noisy." Ishtar sighed then she closed her eyes

After minutes from driving Maria saw the smoke from the towers from far area, she stopped driving and looked at the towers while they were been attacked

"Why did you stop?" Ishtar yelled at her

"I am not going there." Maria seemed afraid

"Why?"

"The police are already evacuating places. We can not reach the towers."

"You have to go. I want to see William." Ishtar kept yelling

"Maybe he is not there."

"Maybe he is there."

"We are far from the towers and I can smell the smoke and see the attack. I am not going there."

"Okay, fine I will go." Ishtar said then she opened her door and got out of the car

"Are you crazy?" Maria said then she got out of the car and ran behind Ishtar. "Listen to me." Maria said when she stood infront of Ishtra "Please listen to me." She held her arms "Maybe William is not there. Maybe he was taking a shower and fell in the tube. Maybe he is still sleeping."

"He called me before."

"Call him again."

"He did not answer."

"You have to check his apartment or call his friend."

"His friend works in the tower."

"Call another friend or his mother."

Ishtar looked at her "I want to go to the towers."

"The towers have been attacked."

"I will go there with you or without you."

"Okay. We will go." Maria said then she sighed. She did what Ishtar wanted also she believed Ishtar was wrong and William is safe and alive. Maria drove for few minutes then she stopped driving. The area was surrounded by reporters and people were looking at the attack or calling on their cell phones.

"I can not drive." Maria said while Ishtar opened the door and ran toward the towers "Wait, I am coming with you." Maria yelled but Ishtar kept running then Maria said herself "I have to follow her. I can not leave her alone." Maria started walking toward the towers but she could not reach Ishtar or see her. Ishtar kept running toward the towers while Maria kept walking toward the towers. Ishtar kept looking at the flame and the smoke while she was thinking in William. She wanted to hug him, kiss him and tell him she wanted to marry him at this moment. After minutes of running Ishtar stopped and tried to catch her breath. She looked at the towers and walked slowly toward them. Suddenly the tower collapsed while Ishtar and other people started running far from the tower. She fell on the ground with others. She was crying while the others were screaming and crying. She was not able to see or breathe. She kept coughing and crying while she was sitting on the ground. She rubbed her face in order to see but the dust was everywhere. She stayed in her spot crying and coughing for minutes. Then she stood up and tried to walk. After few minutes she heard a voice calling her

"Maria I am here." Ishtar yelled

"I can not see you." Maria said

"I am here." Ishtar said then she started coughing

Maria hardly saw her while Ishtar kept calling her. Maria stopped and looked at the ground and saw a woman sitting there

"Ishtar." Maria said

"Maria." Ishtar said while Maria sat beside her crying then Ishtar started crying with her. After short time Maria helped her to stand up and started walking

"There is emergency medical ahead of us they can help you." Maria said

"I do not need any help."

"How do you feel?"

"I am fine." Ishtar said

"Let's leave the place."

"I have to see William."

Maria stopped then she held Ishtar's shoulder "You barely survived the collapse. We have to leave this place." Maria yelled while Ishtar started crying then she sat on the ground "I need to see him."

Maria sat beside her while ambulance car were helping people around them

"We can see his mother or his best friend." Maria suggested while Ishtar said "My eyes are hurting."

"Do you need any treatment?" Maria asked kindly

"No, I just need water."

"Okay, I will bring you water." Maria said then she left Ishtar, who started crying

"We have to leave." Maria said while she was helping Ishtar to drink water

"Okay, let's leave." Ishtar said then she stood up and started walking while Maria was helping her.

As soon as they arrived the building Ishtar went to her apartment. She washed her face and got William's key apartment then she went with Maria to William's apartment. She opened the door panicly and got into the apartment. She checked the room and then the washroom but there was no William

"He is not here, I am right. He is inside the tower." Ishtar was screaming

Maria said kindly "Go and take a shower so we can look after him."

"I do not want to take a shower." Ishtar yelled

"What do you want to do?"

"I am going to call Lisa." Ishtar said then she picked up her phone and called Lisa while Maria was standing beside her looking hopeless

"No answer from her." Ishtar, who was angry and disappointed, said "And William."

"Nothing from William. I told you before."

"Call her again." Maria said

"I am going to see her." Ishtar said

"Okay let's go." Maria said then she walked with Ishtar as fast as they can and got out of the building and headed to Lisa's house. As soon as Lisa opened the door and saw Ishtar infront of her, she hugged her and started crying then they walked inside the house and sat on a couch

"Is your kids here?" Ishtar asked

"They are with my mother upstairs."

"Can you tell me what is happening?" Ishtar asked sadly

"The towers had been attacked." Lisa, who was crying, hardly replied

"Was William inside the tower with Patrick?" Ishtar was so afraid from this question and the answer

"Yes, they were inside the tower when the attack happened. Patrick called me and said William is with him." Lisa stopped and did not continue her sentence and started crying while Ishtar's eyes were full of tears. Maria looked at them then she asked Lisa "How do you know?"

"They were inside...." Lisa said angry

"How do you know?" Maria asked again

Lisa wipped her tears and looked at her "What do you mean?"

"I know your husband works there and William was visiting him but they could be in hospital now."

"What are you talking about? Look at me. I barely survived the collapse." Ishtar said angry

Lisa looked at her and said "You were there."

Ishtar looked at her and said "Yes, I went to see William then the tower collapse."

"You should be optimistic about them." Maria said

"Optimistic! What optimistic? I barely understood my husband when he called me because he was coughing."

"I did not understand everything what William said when he called. It was so noisy." Ishar said sadly

"Patrick said that William was with him.... and then I heard his caughing before his call ended and when I called him back, he did not answer me." Lisa said while she was crying

Ishtar said sadly "I thought William was travelling and called to say goodbye."

"I hope they are somewhere and they will surprise us soon." Maria, who was trying to keep them distracted and not thinking about their men, said

"Or maybe they are under debris with the rest of people." Ishtar said

"They are alive." Maria said while she was holding her tears "Maybe they are in the hospital receiving treatment."

Ishtar looked at her "I hope they are somewhere but not inside the towers."

"In coming days we will know what happened." Maria said

"I can not wait for coming days. I want to know what happened to them now." Lisa said then she added while she was crying and yelling "I watched the attack on television when it happened. It was horrible and unimaginable."

"I went there. I saw the smoke, the firefighter, the medical cars, the scream, people and the collapse." Ishtar said

"Everything was horrible but I have hope and I believe they are coming back to see us." Maria said while Lisa and Ishtar looked at her then she added "We have to wait."

"We wait for what?" Ishtar said

"We can go to the hospital." Maria said

"Which hospital!" Ishtar said

"Any hospital you want." Maria said

"They were inside the towers." Lisa said then she added while she was crying "I know what happened to our men."

Maria looked at the two desperate women and said nothing. Inside that room Maria heard only sound of crying and two desperate women who want to see their men for the last time so they can hug them tightly and never let them go.

"Do you want to call William's mother? Maria asked Ishtar

"Why will i call her?"

"Maybe she knows something."

"We can go to her home if you want." Lisa suggested

"No, I do not want to see her." Ishtar said

"Why?" Maria said

"I am afraid of seeing her." Ishtar sighed

"She may know something about him." Maria said

"I already know what happen to him. Our men were inside the tower." Ishtar was angry

"Well you still have to see her."

"No, I think I want to go home." Ishtar was hopeless

"I can not believe they are not coming home." Lisa said while she was crying. Ishtar looked at her and held her tears while Maria looked at both of them and said "You have to have hope."

"Hope! There is no hope with death." Ishtar said then she added "Let leave so we can grief in silece." Ishtar said then she hugged Lisa and left the house.

She was sad and silent on their way to her apartment and Maria kept comforting her

"I want to be alone." Ishtar said to Maria as soon as they arrived the apartment

"You are going to be alone." Maria said and started following Ishtar

"You are following me." Ishtar said madly then she walked quickly into the building

"Maybe he is inside his cottage." Maria was trying to distracted Ishtar's mind from negative thoughts

Ishtar looked at her "What?"

"Do you want to go there?" Maria suggested in hope to stay longer with Ishtar

Ishtar got into the elevator "No."

"Okay." Maria got into the elevator beside Ishtar

"You have to leave." Ishtar said madly

"I will leave but not now."

Ishtar got into William's apartment followed by Maria, who kept following her then Ishtar got into William's room and slammed the door behind her while Maria just sat on a couch waiting for her. Then after fifteen minutes, Ishtar got out of room crying.

Maria embraced her "You need a shower."

Ishtar looked at her "I need drink."

"Clean your self then you can have a drink." Maria said

"I want drink."

Maria held Ishtar's dusty hair then she held her hand and walked her to the bathtub "Clean yourself. I will go to your apartment and bring you some clothes."

After minutes Ishtar got out of the shower. She wore her clothes and got out of the bathroom and walked to William liquor rack and got a bottle of tequila then she walked back to his room

"What are you doing?" Maria asked while she was following her

"Drinking." Ishtar said then she got into the bed while Maria sat on the edge of the bed

"Do you want to go to William mother's house?"

"No." Ishtar said then she started drinking from the bottle

Maria held the bottle and asked Ishtar, who looked at her "Do you want to stay here?"

"Yes and you can leave."

"Yea I am leaving soon." Maria said sadly and kept watching Ishtar. She felt sad for her. She knew something bad happened to William but she was trying to keep her friend positive "You have to stop drinking. We need to go and look for William later." Maria took the bottle from Ishtar's hand

"He was inside the building." Ishtar said then she tried to get the bottle from Maria's hand

"He may be in the hospital now."

Ishtar looked at her and said sadly "Patrick's office is on the top of the towers and they had been attacked first and it is already destroyed."

"We still do not know what happened to them."

"They are gone." Ishtar said then she grabbed the bottle of drink from Maria's hand and said angry "You have to leave. Your daughter needs you."

"She is alright."

"I am also alright. You can leave."

"I will."

"Leave, I want to be alone." Ishtar was angry and disappointed while Maria looked sadly at her. She grabbed the bottle from Ishtar's hand then she left the room.

After half an hour Ishtar layed down in the bed and started crying while Maria was waiting for her in the kitchen. Then she left the room and ran to the bathroom and closed the door behind her while Maria followed her

"Are you okay?" Maria asked Ishtar while she was waiting her outside of the bathroom. Ishtar did not reply and kept throwing up

"Do you need any thing?" Maria asked while Ishtar got out of the bathroom and walked again to the bedroom "No thanks." Ishtar replied then she closed the door behind her. After more than an hour Maria opened slowly the door and looked at Ishtar then she walked slowly toward her. She looked sadly then said "Ishtar, Ishtar." Ishtar did not respond while Maria sighed then she said "Finally she is sleeping. I can leave her for an hour to see my daughter then I will come back to be with her."

Maria left the room quietly then she left the apartment. After an hour Maria went back to the apartment to check on Ishtar. She walked slowly into the apartment and closed the door behind her then she looked after Ishtar. She checked the room first then she went to the kitchen but she could not find her. She was panic and started looking for Ishtar and calling in har name but there was no respond. Finally she found her lying on the bathroom floor. She tried to wake her up but she did not wake up. In the end Maria called an ambulance. After hours Ishtar woke up when a doctor was checking her

"What happened?" Ishtar, who she was looking at her left hand and saw the feeding tube was connected to her left hand, asked in a weak voice

Maria looked sadly at her "You drank alot of alchohol so you ended up in the hospital." Ishtar closed her eyes then she asked "Anything about William."

"No."

"I know he is dead." Ishtar said while the tears was dropping from her eyes

Maria looked at Ishtar then she sat beside her while Ishtar added "Now I can not see him again or wake up next to him in the morning." Ishtar sighed then she added

"He is gone forever. The only things that I have left are memories."

"You are a strong person." Maria said while she was holding her hand

"No one is able to handle with death." Ishtar said then she looked at Maria "Do you think they will be able to find William's body?"

"I do not know. We can ask later for his body."

"How long do I have to wait?"

"I do not know." Maria said then they kept silent for few minutes "I did not tell your sister about you." Maria said

Ishtar looked at her "Can you tell her now please?"

"Yes, sure." Maria stood up

"Also tell her to spend the night with my mother. I am not going back to the apartment."

"What?" Maria was puzzeled

"After leaving the hospital, I want to go to William's cottage and sleep there."

"Okay." Maria said then she got out of the room

As soon as Ishtar left the hospital, she and Maria headed to the cottage. They arrived at the time that Ishtar wanted which was the sunset time. Although Ishtar asked Maria to leave, Maria followed her and stayed beside her. As soon as she reached the cottage Ishtar sat on a chair in front of the cottage and watched the sunset with a smile while Maria looked at her and smiled. She was looking at the sun how it is disappearing slowly slowly and remembering William, who watched and shared with her these amazing and romantic minutes.

"We shared a kiss after last sunset we watched together now I am alone." Ishtar said sadly while Maria looked at her and sighed

After seconds of silence Maria said "You can watch the sunset with me."

Ishtar looked angry at her and said "You are not William."

"No body can replace him but I am your bestfriend."

"You have to leave. I want to be alone." Ishtar was mad

Maria sighed "Only tonight please. I will leave tomorrow."

"You have to stay with your daughter."

"She is alright." Maria said

Ishtar looked at her and stayed silent for minutes then she stood up and leaned on the front door. She sighed then she opened the door and got into the cottage while Maria was behind her and looking sadly at her.

"I got engaged here." Ishtar said while she was looking at the walls then she added while she was looking at her ring "Now I lost my fiancé and forever." Maria looked sadly at her and did not respond. Ishtar walked slowly into the cottage then she sat on the couch and started touching it then she stood up and went to the bedroom and closed the door behind her while Maria looked sadly at her and left her alone.

RUWAIDA ABD

Ishtar opened William's closet and looked at his clothes then she chose one of his shirt and pants and held them to the bed. She set them on the right side of the bed while she laying down on the left side of the bed beside the clothes. She closed her eyes and smiled. William's smiling iamage came to her mind. She remebred the first time they slept on this bed and the time that she lost her virginity. She closed her eyes and started crying then she took her clothes off and wore William's clothes. After more than half an hour Maria knocked on the door

"Can I come in?" Maria asked when she opened the door

"Yes." Ishtar said while she was sitting on the bed

"You cried, right?" Maria asked

"Yes, I did and this side of pillow is so wet so I have to flip the pillow to another side." Ishtar said sadly while she was was flipping her pillow to another side

"I am hungry and you do not have food in the freezer." Maria said then she added while she was sitting on the bed "Do you want to go outside."

"No, I am not hungry."

"Please, you have to eat."

After seconds of thinking Ishtar said "There is a restaurant near the cottage. You can get food from if you want."

"I want you to come with me."

"I will stay here."

Maria sighed then she got into the bed and sat beside Ishtar

"Do you want to see William's mother?"

"No."

"Why?"

"She loves William so much. She was so happy when I first met her and when we got engaged. I do not think I am able to see her or meet her. It is too hard to see her. She loves William and now William had gone."

"He will always be in our thoughts."

"I will always love him and he will always be with me. I can not get him out of my mind or stop thinking about him." Ishtar and Maria wiped their tears then Ishtar added "I was very selfish with him at the beginning of our relastionship. He was satisfied with me. He was so gentle and unique. I will never meet a man like him."

194

"He was so unique." Maria said sadly

"Every Friday I will sleep in this cottage. I have unforgatable memories here."

"Do you think you will change your mind about seeing William's mother?

"No, I do not have courage to see her."

"You have to see her."

"I am afraid if she does not know yet so I will be the first one to tell her what happened to her son."

"And if she knows."

Ishtar sighed then she said after second of thinking "So we can grieve together. We must have his body." Ishtar stood up

Maria looked at her and stood beside her. Ishtar's words panicked Maria

"You do not have to go." Maria said

"You suggested seeing her."

"Yea, but now I am afraid of losing you."

"I wil see her."

"You are still weak."

"I am alright."

Maria sighed "I am coming with you."

"Okay, we will go together." Ishtar walked toward the door while Maria looked at her then she asked her "You are not going to wear your clothes."

"No, I will stay in William's clothes."

"On our way to William mother's house I will show you the restaurant that I ate with William." Ishtar and Maria walked together and got out of the room

Maria looked sadly at her "You still remember them."

"Oh, yea I can also tell you what we ate." Ishtar said sadly then she added "I remember everything he did for me." Ishtar could not keep her eyes dry "I told you he was very unique."

Maria was helping Ishtar while they were walking to the car then she opened the door for her and helped her to got into the car. On their way Ishtar started crying as soon as they passed a restaurant that she ate her favourite meal with William, and then she smiled when she was saying "I danced with him for first time." Then she covered her face and said while she was crying "There will be no more Valentine's day and birthday gift only tears and pain." Maria looked at Ishtar, who was experience intense grief as she mourn her loss and stopped the car "I am returning back to the cottage."

"No." Ishtar was angry

Maria looked at her while she was taking a deep breath "Okay, we will see her." although Maria did not agree with Ishtar but she did not want her best friend to feel she is alone as she mourns her loss. After they reach William mother's house, William's younger brother told them that his mother is in hospital because she collapsed after she learned from Lisa that William was with Patrick inside the tower when the attack happened

"Do you want to return here in another day?" Maria asked Ishtar when they got into the car

"There will be no more another day. Everyday will be same as previous day." Ishtar said then she added "Please stop at floral shop. I want to buy some flowers."

Maria looked at her smiling "Sure."

"And I need candles."

"Candles! Why?" Maria was surprised

"I want them."

"Okay we will buy what ever you want." Maria agreed but she seemed confused

"Thanks."

As soon as they saw a floral shop, Maria stopped and then they got into the shop

"I hope I can find the same flowers that William bought." Ishtar said happily while she was looking at the flowers

Maria was shock "You want to buy same flowers as your fiancé bought."

"Yes."

"Is it the same thing with the candles?"

"Yes." Ishtar said then she walked far from Maria and started looking for the flowers that William bought for her while Maria looked sadly at her. As soon as Ishtar found the flowers, she smiled and held them tightly

"Did yoy find them?" Maria, who was standing behind Ishtar, asked

"Yes, now we can leave because I am so tired."

"Okay, but can I buy food later"

"Yes, you can buy but I will stay inside the car."

"Okay." Maria said warmly then they got out of the shop "What about the candles?" Maria asked

"I want to buy the same that they were when William proposed to me."

"Okay, we will buy anything you want."

During their way to the cottage Ishtar was holding the flowers in her hands and kept silent while Maria was watching her carefully and hoping to see her bestfreind always beside her. As soon as they reached to cottage, Ishtar lit the candles in the bedroom then she layed into the bedroom with flowers while Maria stayed in the living room eating. In early moning of the next day, Ishtar woke up early to go to the washroom. She looked at the another side of the bed she saw Maria was sleeping beside her while the flowers were on the night table beside her and the candles were blowed out. She tried to get up but she felt so weak. When she tried again, she fell on the floor

"Are you alright?" Maria, who woke up afraid, asked

"No, I am not."

Maria ran to her and helped her to sit again on the bed "You are weak and you are neglecting yourself and did not take your medicine."

"I do not want to take any medicine."

"You have to take care of yourself." Maria was angry and was holding Ishtar's shoulders

"Why do I have to take care of myself?" Ishtar yelled "I just lost my fiancé."

"Because your fiancé take care of you and he always wants to see you happy and healthy." Maria said then she sighed and looked at her while she was standing "He always wants to see happy. He sacrificed himself for you."

"Yes, he did and I can not live without him."

"Yes, you can. You have to force yourself because you have to keep his memories alive and you can not keep them if you are dead."

"But it is hard." Ishtar said while she crying

"I know it is hard but you have too." Maria said while her eyes were full of tears then she added "Do you want to see the sunrise as a new beginning?"

Ishtar looked at her "Okay."

Maria smiled then she helped Ishtar to walk to outside the cottage so they can see the sunrise

"You need a cane." Maria suggested while she was helping Ishtar to sit

"No, I do not."

"You should get your mother's cane." Maria said while she was sitting beside Ishtar.

"I do not need a cane."

"Really."

"Yes." Ishtar said then they watched the sunrise silently and smiling

"What do you want to eat for breakfast?" Maria asked Ishtar

Ishtar looked at her "I do not know."

"A breakfast that William loved." Maria said in hope to make Ishtar eats

"But we have an empty fridge." Ishtar said

Maria smiled and said happily "Do not worry I bought everthing last night."

Ishtar seemed excited and started counting "eggs, waffles, sausage and coffee."

Maria smiled and said while she was standing "Okay, everything will be ready in half an hour." Then held Ishtar's arm and helped her to walk

"Where do you want to eat?" Maria asked after they got into the cottage

"In the kitchen." Ishtar replied then she said while she was sitting on the chair "Can I get the flowers and the candles here, please?"

"Yes." Maria said then she left the kitchen room

"Do you need something else?" Maria, who was carring the candles and flowers, asked Ishtar when she entered the kitchen room and saw Ishtar was trying to stand

"I feel cold." Ishtar said

"I will bring one of William's jacket."

"Yes, please." Ishtar said then she sat again in her seat while Maria lighted the candles and set the flowers beside Ishtar then she left the kitchen. After few minutes Maria came back with a jacket in her hands then she said while she was giving the jacket to Ishtar "Now I can prepare breakfast."

"You should leave. You have to see your daughter."

"She is alright. Today her father is taking care of her."

"I am sorry for causing all these complications for you."

Maria looked at her "You are my best friend and I will do anything for you." Ishtar smiled and said nothing while Maria continued preparing the breakfast

"Now we can eat." Maria said while she was setting the plates on the table "And then you have to take your medicine." Maria gave the medicine for Ishtar

"Okay, I will."

"How many times have you been in this cottage?" Maria asked Ishtar when she was sitting on a chair to eat

"Five times."

"You never came alone, right!"

"No." Ishtar said then she started eating

"Do you still cold?" Maria asked

"No, I am fine."

"By the way you look great in the photo album."

"What photo album?" Ishtar was surprise

"Yesterday after you slept I stayed awake and started discovering the cottage then I found photo albums."

"Can I see the photo albums, please?" Ishtar was surprise

"Sure you can." Maria said then she stood up and left the kitchen room. When she came back, she was smiling and holding the photo album

"Thanks." Ishtar said when she held the album. She seemed excited and started opening the album and watching the pictures. Some of them were William's pictures with his friends, in the other he was with his mother and his sibling. His pictures have different occasions. In the end of the album it was their pictures together during their time in the cottage. She sighed and closed the album and started crying

"Why are you crying?" Maria said while she was taking the album back

"I miss him. It is so hard living without him."

"I know." Maria said sadly and blamed herself for bringing the album and making her best friend devastated then she added "Later we can get out and eat in the restaurant that you ate with William."

"Okay, now I went to go back to the room."

"Please continue eating."

"I am not hungry any more." Ishtar stood up

"You have to take your medicine." Maria said after she stood beside her

"Okay, I will go to the washroom first then I will come back."

"I am coming with you."

"No, I can go alone." Ishtar said

"No, you can not." then they walked together to the bathroom. As soon as she opened the door, she looked at the shower's curtain and remembered the first that she showered with William then she looked at her right side and opened the cabinet. She found on shelves William's razor, shaving cream, after-shave lotion, and razor blades. She looked sadly at them and then she touched them "Everything here belongs to you." She said then she closed her eyes and said "Why did you leave me so early?" She leaned on the wall and started crying then after seconds she heard Maria's calling her

"Are you okay?"

Ishtar wipped her tears and said "Yes, I am."

"Okay I am waiting you here infront of the door."

"Okay, I am coming."

After few minutes Ishtar got out of the washroom while Maria held her and walked together to the kitchen room then Ishtar sat on a chair while Maria gave her the medicine

"Do you still feel cold?" Maria asked

"No, I am better now." Ishtar said then she added "You should see your daughter."

"I will see her later. Your sister called while you were in the washroom."

"What did she want?"

"She is asking about you."

"She is with my mother, right?"

"Yes, she is but she wants to come here and see you."

"No, she has to stay with my mother."

Maria looked at her and sighed "What about you? You do not want to go back to the apartment."

Ishtar looked at her "I do not know."

"What do you mean by you do not know?"

"I will decide later."

"You mother and your sister need you."

Ishtar looked at her and said after thinking "Okay, I will go back."
"When?"
"After sunset."
Maria smiled "Okay." Then she asked her after seconds of silence "We can eat lunch in one of restaurants you used to eat with William."
Ishtar looked at her "I did not even celebrate one year anniversary with him."
Maria looked at her then she said after seconds of thinking "How do you want to celebrate it?"
"What?"
"Tell me your plan."
Ishtar looked at her and said after hesitation "A cake."
"And."
"Ofcourse I will buy flowers, candles and coming to the cottage to watch the sunset."
"Okay, good. What else?"
"Drinking." Ishtar said with a smile
Although the word drinking panicked Maria but she said nothing about it because she was trying to get her bestfriend from the bottom of the disaster that she was. She knows Ishtar is lonely, miserable and has suicidal thoughts but the only way that rescue Ishtar is to keep doing what she did with William, who is gone forever and she has to be with her so she can lead her to the safe side and pull her from the bottom
"What do you want to wear a dress or William's clothes?"
Ishtar looked at Maria and said with a smile "A dress."
"Okay, I believe we have to prepare for it." Maria said with a smile
"Yes, we will. I have to see William's mother also so we can get William's body."
Maria looked at her then she said after seconds of silence "Okay, we will see her after seeing your mother and sister."
"Okay, good."
"How do you feel now?"
"Still weak."
"Do you want to have some rest in the bed?"
"Yes, please." Ishtar said while she was nodding her head. Maria stood up and helped Ishtar to stand up then they walked together to William's room.

Printed in the USA
CPSIA information can be obtained
at www.ICGtesting.com
LVHW092031250624
783963LV00002B/215